CLASSICS OF FANTASTIC LITERATURE

or,

LES ÉPINES NOIRES

SELECTED REVIEW ESSAYS

by

Robert Reginald

and

Douglas Menville

BORGO PRESS
an imprint of Wildside Press
2005

Borgo Literary Guides
ISSN 0891-9623
Number Three

ISBN 0-8095-0918-0 (hardcover)
ISBN 0-8095-1918-6 (paperback)

Published in the United States of America by
The Borgo Press, an imprint of Wildside Press
www.wildsidepress.com

FIRST EDITION

CONTENTS

DEDICATION

FOR BARRY R. LEVIN,

Something of a Classic Himself!

And in Memory of

ARNOLD ZOHN
(1905-1985)

INTRODUCTION

THE ARNOLD ZONE

Once upon a time, there was a man named Arnold Zohn who had an idea for a new publishing line. He would publish a series of hardbound reprints of classic nonfiction works of the past to sell to all of the new academic libraries being created during the 1960s. He would package them together in series of 25-50 volumes each, edited by well-known academics, and he would then make his fortune.

He was able to sell the idea to The New York Times Company, and Arno Press was born, ostensibly named for the Arno River in Florence, Italy (but really for Arnold!). To run this new enterprise, Zohn hired Harry McConnell as Editor-in-Chief, and soon Arno was republishing hundreds of volumes annually for the library market, in expensive editions averaging 250 copies. The company was successful from its very inception.

In 1974 we sent a proposal to Arno Press for a reprint series of fiction and nonfiction volumes devoted to classic science fiction, pointing out that no such series had ever been published to that date. The books would be jointly edited by Reginald, then working on a bibliography of SF for Gale Research, and his good friend and fellow bibliophile, Douglas Menville, whose personal knowledge (and equally large collection) of fantastic literature were unsurpassed.

A contract was issued immediately, and *Science Fiction: 62 Books* was published in April of 1975. A second series, *Supernatural & Occult Fiction: 63 Books*, appeared in 1976, and a third collection of titles, *Lost Race & Adult Fantasy Fiction: 69 Books*, in 1978. A fourth series reprinting short and long nonfiction works about SF and fantasy was sold to Arno in 1978, and the editorial work actually completed; but Arno very suddenly succumbed to the constriction of the library market in the early 1980s, and the volumes were never published.

After Arno's collapse and sale to the Ayer Company, Arnold Zohn retired to his estate on Long Island, where he founded a small personal imprint, Sagapress, and also did some consultation work for other academic imprints. He agreed to publish twenty of the books slated for the SF criticism series, and even applied for Cataloging-in-Publication records from the Library of Congress, but suddenly died in 1985 before the anthologies could be released. The volumes then vanished into the æther of Never-Was and Never-Where and Never-Were.

As part of our work for Arno, we wrote all of the advertising copy for the three series, each of which had its own, separately published slick brochure of roughly 15-20 pages. These included detailed descriptions and plot summaries for all of the 194 volumes comprising the three sets, books for which very little hard information is available in any other source.

Classics of Fantastic Literature reorganizes all of this data into one alphabet, arranged by the name of the author or editor, plus a detailed author/title index. Some of the records have been updated or rewritten slightly, but we have mostly not attempted to add any additional critical apparatus beyond what was included with the original descriptions. We hope that the historian of fantastic literature will still find something of value here.

We want to thank John Betancourt for agreeing to publish this volume, and to express our gratitude to the late Arnold Zohn and the late Harry McConnell for their willingness to take on two untried series editors. We both had an enormously good time playing with these books.

—Robert Reginald & Douglas Menville
San Bernardino & North Hollywood, CA
31 July 2004

CLASSICS OF FANTASTIC LITERATURE

About, Edmond, translated by Henry Holt. *The Man with the Broken Ear.* New York: Leypoldt & Holt, 1867.
Man has always been fascinated by the possibility of suspending life for an extended period of time. Edmond About handles this theme with remarkable realism. The time is 1813. Pierre Victor Fougas, a colonel in the French army under Napoleon, has been captured by the Russians while on a spy mission. Sentenced to be executed, he freezes into a coma during a particularly vicious winter night, and is near death when found by Dr. Meiser, whom the Russians have been using as a translator. Meiser, an expert on the desiccation and resuscitation of lower forms of animal life, decides that the only hope for the colonel is to remove all his body fluids, and leave his restoration to future scientists.

Since the soldier will be killed in any case, Meiser certifies his death, and buys the "body" for experimental use. The body is carefully dried out and packed into a special coffin; and when the doctor dies in 1824, his will specifies the processes needed to bring the Frenchman back to life. But Meiser's nephew is troubled by a provision in the will leaving the doctor's vast estate to the colonel, and he destroys the special instructions, claiming the money as next heir.

The body is sold to a junk dealer. Then in 1859 Léon Renault, an engineer, finds the casket in a pawn shop, and buys it as a curiosity. The history of the corpse is traced, and Léon and several colleagues decide to try a restoration. The colonel is revived by carefully reintroducing his body fluids, and the flamboyant soldier immediately sets out to seduce Léon's fiancée, Clementine, who bears a remarkable resemblance to the colonel's lover of 1813. The soldier petitions the new Emperor, Napoléon III, for reinstatement with his regiment, but is refused because of his legal age (now over seventy). This, combined with the astonishing revelation that Clementine is his granddaughter, proves a heavy blow, and the gallant Frenchman is found dead in a hotel room, just one month after resuscitation. And while the official autopsy indicates severe disorders resulting from desiccation, the unofficial verdict is a broken heart.

Ainsworth, W(illiam) Harrison. *Auriol; or, The Elixir of Life.* London: George Routledge & Sons, 1865.

In the closing hours of the sixteenth century, Dr. Lamb discovers an extraordinary elixir of life. But, just as he is about to quaff the mixture, the centenarian has a heart seizure, and dies before he can save himself. His great-grandson, Auriol Darcy, steals the potion and drinks it himself, thereby becoming immortal. Two centuries later, in 1830, the story resumes, as Darcy, still young in form, is assaulted by robbers and left for dead. His marvelous resilience asserts itself, and within a few days, he is completely healed again. He falls in love with his beautiful nurse, Ebba Thorneycroft, but renounces her after a mysterious stranger insists that he fulfill an unspecified bargain.

Years before, Cyprian de Rougemont had made a pact with the devil to give the fiend Darcy's soul in exchange for unlimited wealth. The Frenchman then seduced the poverty-stricken immortal with a similar compact: prosperity and position for Darcy, and a female victim for de Rougemont every ten years. Darcy, desperate for money, had signed the agreement, and his fiancée of the time, Edith Talbot, was seized by the monster on the night of their wedding. Now, thirty years later, the cycle has replayed itself, and de Rougemont has taken Auriol's current lover, the girl Ebba.

Darcy pursues the fiend to his hiding place, a decaying castle, but is captured by the Frenchman and locked away in a cell. All appears lost when Ebba apparently signs an agreement giving her soul to the devil. Cyprian then torments the youth further by appearing before him in sixteenth-century clothing, claiming that Darcy has been insane and is only now recovering his mind. Darcy is shown a replica of Lamb's old laboratory, and the centenarian himself suddenly appears to greet him. The story ends with Auriol convinced of his own mental instability.

Included with this novel are two short stories, "The Old London Merchant" and "A Night's Adventure in Rome."

Allen, Grant. *The British Barbarians: A Hill-Top Novel.* London: John Lane, 1895.

This satire of Victorian mores and times begins with the appearance of a stranger in a British suburb. "Mr. Bertram Ingledew" his card says, and although he speaks excellent English, he is completely ignorant, it seems, of the local customs and taboos, as he calls them. Inquiries about his origins are politely turned aside, but he is obviously well-to-do, and Philip Christy, the first person to see the man, helps integrate him into British society. However, it is Philip's married sister, Frida Monteith, whom the "Alien" finds interesting, and his frank and open admiration of the woman draws a quick response.

Bertram persuades his paramour to leave her husband, and run off with him to Heymoor, where he says they must wait a few days until he can arrange to take her with him to his "home." But Robert Monteith discovers the lovers on the moor, and shoots Ingledew in cold blood. A faint blue flame issues from the wound, and forms into a wraith hanging in the air, growing thicker and thicker as the body beneath it dissolves into nothingness. As Bertram vanishes, he says: "I forgot with what manner of savage I had still to deal. And now I must go back once more to the place whence I came—to the twenty-fifth century."

Ames, Joseph Bushnell. *The Bladed Barrier.* New York: Century, 1929.

This was the last novel to be completed before the untimely death of this popular Western novelist, and is quite different from the usual run of his fiction. Rick Stillman and Jimmy Cavanaugh are young prospectors who have become discouraged by a run of bad luck, until the sudden discovery of a murdered Mexican starts them off on the strangest adventure of their lives. The Mexican, dying from multiple stab wounds, clutches in his fist a huge emerald of exquisite design and manages to gasp out whispered words about "treasure—fiends—a serpent—the gate of swords" before he expires. Together with a third friend, "Tex" Ripley, the boys decide to go in search of the treasure beyond the sinister "Boca Infierno" in the barren wasteland of Baja California.

After a grueling journey through the deserts of Lower California, they locate the ominous "Hell's Mouth" in an obsidian canyon and emerge into an incredible hidden valley beyond. They are seized by strange hooded priests who take them to the lost city of an ancient Chinese civilization. The sadistic ruler, a Chinese mandarin named Li-Kiang, threatens the boys with torture and death unless they produce the emerald, which Rick has hidden. When they refuse, the mandarin forces them to witness a hideous ceremony in which a man is fed alive to the gigantic serpent-god of the people. The ceremony is presided over by a captive white girl, Phyllis Brooks, who is forced to serve as priestess. Phyllis casts her lot with the boys, and with her help they are able to escape, kill the Chinese leader, and pass through the terrible Gate of Swords—the "bladed barrier" to the outside world—with a fortune in emeralds.

Anderson, Olof W. *The Treasure Vault of Atlantis: Giving an Account of a Very Remarkable Discovery of an Ancient Temple of Wealth Built and Concealed within a Mountain of Rock Amidst Tropical Jungle by a People of a Forgotton Civilization That Existed Before the Great Flood; Also a Record of the Mysterious Messages That Seemed to Come from a Supernatural Source That Led to the Very Wonderful Adventures and the Fascinating Story of a Great Love Related Herein.* Minneapolis: Midland Publishing Co., 1925.

The narrator has a vision in which the voice of the gods tells him to seek a treasure to find himself. For it seems that in a previous incarnation he was the ruler of Atlantis, and had been told by his counselors that the end of that island state was probable within the near future. It had been determined that, in order to save something from the advanced civilization they had built, a great mountain would be hallowed out and filled with artifacts, as well as several leading citizens preserved in a trance state. The author seeks help from a wealthy baron, and they mount an expedition to the Amazon.

After weeks of struggling through swamps and jungles, they spy a strange mountain formation in the distance, like a giant woman reclining on her back. The nearer they come, the more pronounced the structure seems. In the side of the cliff is a cave entrance, perfectly hollowed out into a cube. With luck and experimentation they discover the secret of the cave, and enter the vast caverns carved out within. In the middle of one of these rooms, they find a man perfectly preserved inside a glass case.

Following an illustrated book of instructions, they revive the Atlantean (for such he proves to be), and he in turn revives the fifty or sixty others of his race. The men of Atlantis have marvelous scientific instruments, including a helicopter-like flying machine and an advanced television system that will reveal any part of the globe, merely by adjusting its dials. Among other things, they invent (at the narrator's request) a means of communicating with the dead. With life after death proven beyond any doubt, the millennium is at hand, and the treasures of the vault are set aside until the new Atlantis has become a reality.

Anstey, F. *Humour & Fantasy: Vice Versa, The Tinted Venus, A Fallen Idol, The Talking Horse, Salted Almonds, The Brass Bottle.* London: John Murray, 1931.

Thomas Anstey Guthrie, who wrote under the pseudonym "F. Anstey," was a tremendously successful British humorist during the late 1800s and early 1900s, with dozens of novels, short stories, plays, parodies, and humorous essays to his credit. Unlike many of his contemporaries, who occasionally strayed into humorous fantasy, Anstey made this area his own, breaking away from conventional ghost stories and developing new and ingenious situations drawn from various legendary and classical sources.

Anstey can be called the father of the modern humorous fantasy novel, developed and made world famous in the 1920s and 1930s by Thorne Smith (whose *Turnabout* is merely a variation on Anstey's *Vice Versa*), and brought to fruition in John W. Campbell's superb magazine, *Unknown (Worlds)*, in the 1940s. Here, writers such as L. Sprague de Camp and Fletcher Pratt, L. Ron Hubbard, Robert Bloch, Henry Kuttner, and many others produced an unparalleled array of fantastic fun.

Sadly, even though many plays and motion pictures were made from his works, Anstey is almost completely unknown today, especially in the United States. When the present omnibus edition was first published in 1931, just three years before Anstey's death, the bulk of his work was already out-of-print and forgotten, except for *Vice Versa* (1882), his first novel and the most successful. Six of his best books are assembled here, four novels and two books of short stories and playlets.

Vice Versa tells of the exchange of personalities between a schoolboy and his overbearing father. *The Tinted Venus* (1885) details the amorous entanglements of a young man who finds himself engaged to the goddess Aphrodite incarnated in a statue. *A Fallen Idol* (1886) deals with a malignant Indian idol's torment of a young painter. *The Talking Horse* (1891) is just that. *Salted Almonds* (1906) is a collection of short stories and playlets. *The Brass Bottle* (1900), suggested by Arabian Nights tales, is the original of the often-imitated story of the young man who discovers an Arabian *djinn* in an old bottle.

Arlen, Michael. *Ghost Stories*. London: William Collins Sons, 1932.

Michael Arlen, whose name was originally Dikran Kouyoumdjian, was a popular Armenian-British writer during the 1920s and '30s. Although his fantasy output was small, he did pen a number of remarkable supernatural tales, the best of which are included in this collection.

"The Prince of the Jews" tells how two rivals forgot their animosities after their mutual departures from earthly life. "The Gentleman from America" is scared into a madhouse by the ghost haunting an old mansion. A young boy meets his future lover in a vision in a lovely story called "To Lamoir." "The Ghoul of Golders Green" is the story of phantoms created by a motion picture company.

"The Ancient Sin" tells how a vile murder is recreated again and again and again by the spirits of the participants. A gentleman takes a shortcut through a dark alleyway early in the morning, and engages in a conversation with "The Loquacious Lady of Lansdowne Passage;" unfortunately, the clock strikes three, and the old crone vanishes, having remembered her murder of many years ago. "The Smell in the Library" tells of a vengeance reaching beyond the grave.

Arnold, Edwin Lester. *Lepidus the Centurion: A Roman of To-Day*. London: Cassell & Co., 1901.

Edwin Lester Arnold, the son of Sir Edwin Arnold, is best known for his classic tale of immortality, *The Wonderful Adventures of Phra the Phoenician* (1890), a book which has had many editions and which influenced such writers as George Griffith, Edgar Rice Burroughs and Jack London. His 1905 novel, *Lieut. Gullivar Jones: His Vacation*, is an early interplanetary novel of heroic adventures on Mars, also thought by some to have influenced Burroughs.

Between *Phra* and *Gulliver* Arnold wrote another novel dealing with immortality, *Lepidus the Centurion*, in which a Victorian English squire named Louis Allanby stumbles upon the ancient tomb of a Roman centurion named Marcus Lepidus. Allanby discovers that the Roman is not dead, but in a state of suspended animation, and by infusing part of his own vitality into the sleeper, he manages to bring Lepidus to life! The Roman rapidly adapts to his new environment and Allanby brings him home, passing him off as a distant relative from the Italian branch of the family.

The tone of this novel is that of a romantic comedy, much lighter than Arnold's other works; however, conflict develops when Lepidus falls in love with Allanby's fiancée, Pris Smith, whom the Roman recognizes as the incarnation of his love of centuries ago. The competition becomes heated between the two men, although a measure of friendship is retained, until they decide to duel to the death with rapiers for Pris. But she stops them, so Lepidus proposes a desperate final solution: each man will plead his case to Pris, and the loser will drink poison. Pris chooses Louis, and Lepidus returns to his eternal sleep in the ancient tomb.

Arnold, Edwin Lester. *Lieut. Gullivar Jones: His Vacation.* London: S. C. Brown, Langham, 1905.

Gullivar Jones, USN, finds a battered old carpet near the body of a stranger while walking one night in New York City. He wishes himself on Mars, and before he can realize what has happened the carpet rolls over him and lifts into the air. Jones is unceremoniously dumped near the large Martian city of Seth, where a native teaches him the language telepathically.

The Martians he sees are the degenerate remains of a once-flourishing civilization that ruled the planet in eons past, but now have been reduced to small territories by barbarian incursions. The people are simple-minded, forgetful, totally devoted to the emotions and pleasures of the moment, and incapable of violence. Each year the barbarian Thithers come for their tribute, and this season they take with them the Princess Heru, whom Jones loves.

The sailor sets out to rescue his lover, but is carried up the River of the Dead, accompanied by hundreds of rafts bearing Martian bodies. Unable to land on the sheer river banks, Jones is swept many miles into the frozen north, where the great river disappears into a large cave. He jumps for a ledge at the last possible moment, and manages to find his way out of the wastes, which border on the barbarian realm. After many adventures in the wilderness, Jones arrives at the palace of King Arhap, who is holding the girl captive.

The sailor and his princess escape from the savages during a meteor strike, and return to the fairy city of Seth.

But Arhap has followed with his legions, and the city is attacked and destroyed; the Martian inhabitants have forgotten how to resist. Heru flees with her handmaidens, and Jones finds his carpet in the great storage room where he is besieged. Just as the barbarians break through the door, he wishes himself in New York, and the carpet returns him to his native planet unharmed.

Some researchers believe this novel was the inspiration for Edgar Rice Burroughs's Martian series.

Atkins, Frank, writing as Frank Aubrey. *The Devil-Tree of El Dorado: A Novel*. London: Hutchinson, 1896.

Frank Aubrey was the author of a number of successful volumes of science fiction in the late 1800s and early 1900s, the most popular of which proved to be the lost-race classic, *The Devil-Tree of El Dorado*. Although published two years before Aubrey's *A Queen of Atlantis* (recent scholarship has revealed that *Queen* was published a year earlier than previously thought, *i.e.*, in 1898), *Devil-Tree* is actually a loose sequel to the former novel, continuing the adventures of the strange, godlike Monella.

Claiming to possess ancient documents pertaining to the legendary Spanish city of El Dorado, Monella leads an expedition which includes two adventurous young men, Jack Templemore and Leonard Elwood, into the jungles of British Guiana. Monella claims that this city, actually named Manoa, is located atop a vast plateau called Roraima. After hazardous adventures with poisonous snakes and wild tigers, the trio reach the base of the seemingly impenetrable mountain, but, aided by the ancient documents, Monella finds an entrance. Inside is a verdant valley with strange flowers and animals—and the golden city of Manoa!

The party arrives just in time to save the life of Ulama, daughter of the king of Manoa. The king of the white, non-Indian inhabitants of the city welcomes the explorers with gratitude, but warns them against the evil and rebellious faction of the city, led by the high priest Coryon, who offers human sacrifices to a huge man-eating tree! Monella takes command of the king's forces, and after a terrific battle, the priests are overthrown and the devil-tree destroyed. Monella reveals that he is actually the legendary, 2,000-year-old leader of the Manoans, returned to fulfill an ancient prophecy after centuries of wandering in the outside world.

Atkins, Frank, writing as Frank Aubrey. *King of the Dead: A Weird Romance.* London: John Macqueen, 1903.

This extraordinarily rare novel was originally published in 1903 but most of the printing was accidentally destroyed in a flood; perhaps ten or twenty copies have survived to modern times.

Arnold Neville is approached by Don Lorenzo, an unusual Brazilian, to lead an expedition into the South American interior. When he refuses to accept, Lorenzo kidnaps his fiancée and her mother and challenges Neville to follow him. Arnold and his friend, Gordon Leslie, charter a boat to British Guiana, and there follow a trail into the tropical jungles. While camped near the river, Leslie decides to make a side trip to explore a mythical "Haunted Mountain," and encounters the enchanting girl, Rhelma, and her father, Manzoni, a scientist who has spent twenty years on the mountain.

Manzoni, it seems, had once lived in a fabulous city not far away, where the remnant of a master race still survives. Lorenzo, or Lyostrah, is the leader of this people, and is determined to reestablish its supremacy on the earth. Manzoni, the hereditary king, had refused to play along with Lyostrah's schemes and was then exiled to his lonely hideaway.

Leslie returns to camp and accompanies his friend to Myrvonia, the capital, where the two lovers are reunited. Lyostrah wants Neville for his second-in-command, but the Englishman refuses to comply. Meanwhile, strange things are happening as ogres from the Temple of Dornanda, a huge, rocky fortress in the center of the land, are killing the people during the night and eating their flesh. The archpriestess Alloyah is jealous of Lyostrah's interest in Arnold's fiancée, and has used her powers to reanimate the dead.

But Manzoni returns, and together with a chastised Lyostrah summons the powers of the heavens; the mindless creatures of Alloyah are destroyed, and the priestess herself is torn to pieces by her monsters. Lyostrah dies courageously, and Manzoni is restored to his wise rule over the people.

Atkins, Frank, writing as Frank Aubrey. *A Queen of Atlantis: A Romance of the Caribbean Sea.* London: Hutchinson, 1898.

The Atlantis myth has fascinated men for over two thousand years, but at no time has it received more attention than at the beginning of the last century. One of the better books dealing with this theme is Aubrey's *Queen of Atlantis.*

A group of four Americans on a Caribbean cruise is marooned in the mysterious Sargasso Sea by a mutinous crew. After several dangerous encounters with assorted sea monsters, they discover the hidden island of Atlantis, peopled by a race of men living in beauty and splendor, just as they did thousands of years ago, when Atlantis was a mighty empire. The Atlanteans welcome the party, hailing the American heroine, Vanina, as their long-awaited Queen. Monella, the god-like stranger who has become the leader of Atlantis, seeks the Americans' help in defeating the forces of neighboring Karanda, who have invaded the island under the aegis of King Kara. The vanquished monarch uses his powers to bewitch Vanina into a promise of marriage, and then puts her into a deep coma resembling death.

Owen Wydale, her sweetheart, seeks help elsewhere on the island, and comes upon a strange, elf-like race of flying creatures called the "Flower-Dwellers"; he persuades them to provide an antidote after saving the daughter of their ruler. Kara orders the two Americans sacrificed to a birdlike monster, but Monella rescues them and slays both beast and king with the powerful gas-weapon of the birdmen. With peace restored, the two lovers and Vanina's brothers leave the lost island to return to civilization.

This was the second of three novels by Aubrey (Atkins) featuring Monella, the others being *The Devil-Tree of Eldorado* (1896) and *King of the Dead* (1903).

17

Atkins, Frank, writing as Fenton Ash. *A Trip to Mars*. London: W. & R. Chambers, 1909.

A culture may sometimes be judged better by what it produces for its children and adolescents than for its adult population. This novel is typical of the juvenile fiction of its day, having been penned by a prolific author, Frank Atkins, who also wrote SF under the name Frank Aubrey, Gerald Wilton, and Jack Lawford

Two orphans are spending a year with a scientist named Armoath on a lonely island totally uninhabited save for themselves and several retainers. Suddenly a giant meteorite crashes into the sea near the island. Upon investigation, the boys find a giant, egg-shaped spacecraft floating on the water. A hatch opens, and several persons in gaudy dress appear on the platform; one suddenly faints, and falls into the water. Gerald immediately dives overboard, and pulls the man out of the water.

The Martian King, for such he turns out to be, offers the boys and their guardian a trip back to his own planet, and they gladly accept. Upon their arrival, the king introduces them to his son, Prince Alondra, and gives him the task of showing their visitors the Martian civilization. Martian culture is heavily dependent on air travel, both by airship and by personal flight through motorized and unpowered wings that can be attached to one's back.

The boys quickly become proficient in using these devices. King Ivanta has brought back from Earth several pouches filled with diamonds, which are unknown on Mars; one of his client kings, covetous of the gems, revolts against his overlord, and tries to seize the prince as a hostage. But the king, his son, and the men from Earth throw back the assault in a great aerial battle, and the rebels are captured or killed. Gerald and Jack return to Earth with the diamonds, which will henceforth be forbidden on Mars, and bid farewell to their friends with the promise of future adventures in space awaiting them.

Balzac, Honoré de, writing as Horace de Saint-Aubin. *The Centenarian; or, The Two Beringhelds (Le centenaire;*

ou, les deux Beringhelds), translated from the original 1822 French edition by George Edgar Slusser. New York: Arno Press, 1976.

Early in his prolific career, the great French writer Balzac published a number of popular novels under various pseudonyms. This is the first English translation of a gothic novel that is a stunning *tour-de-force* of supernatural horror.

M. Beringheld has made a pact with the devil, whereby he has received immortality and occult powers in exchange for the soul of a young girl freely given each hundred years. Every century Beringheld must locate a gullible wench, kill her, and inject her life fluids into his own veins. The old man has remarkable talents: he can pass through walls, and travel great distances within a few hours; his presence in Jaffa at the time of Napoléon brings a sudden halt to the plague raging there. And he can seemingly raise the dead. In his look and on his brow one reads the power and misery of this curse of long life.

General Tullius Beringheld, the last descendant of the old man, feels compelled by what he has already heard to tell what he knows. His journal relates the strange events surrounding the immortal's life. But the story is abruptly interrupted when the evil man abducts Tullius's fiancée and takes her to the catacombs of the castle. Old Beringheld is preparing to sacrifice the girl to his lust for eternal life, when his young relative appears on the scene and vanquishes the forces of the devil.

Balzac patterned this novel after Charles Maturin's *Melmoth the Wanderer,* a popular gothic work of the time, but exaggerated all the existing conventions and added new ones for spice. The scientific interests of Balzac's day are all visible in his machinery of horror; rather than use science to explain away the supernatural, he makes it serve the deeper cause of mystery, uncertainty, and chilling horror.

Beale, Charles Willing. *The Secret of the Earth*. London: F. Tennyson Neely, 1899.

The Secret of the Earth combines several themes common to turn-of-the-century science fiction: the inner Earth theory, anti-gravity devices, and the use of the lost

19

manuscript device to lend credence to the story. Two American brothers, Torrence and Guthrie Attlebridge, journey to Britain to seek financing for their new anti-gravity airship, which they intend to use in exploring the mysteries of the North Pole. After finding sufficient financial help to build the craft, they set sail on a northward course, and discover an unknown sea, beyond which lies the entrance to the strange world inside the Earth. Here they find a vast fortune in treasure, great ruins, and many other relics of an ancient lost civilization. The primitive remnants of this dying people believe the two explorers to be gods, and give them a royal welcome to the hidden world.

Continuing their journey, the Attlebridges are forced to cross a deadly ocean of fire, and must land their damaged airship on a barren desert nearby. They are rescued by huge, roc-like birds directed by a group of mysterious old men inhabiting a desert monastery. With the help of the giant birds, the brothers repair their ship, and leave the inner world through its South Polar opening. Shortly thereafter, their craft fails again, and they find themselves marooned on an unknown island in the South Pacific. Hoping they will be rescued, they write the story of their incredible adventures on their remaining paper, and seal it into a cask which is cast into the ocean.

Beck, L. Adams. *The Ninth Vibration, and Other Stories.* New York: Dodd, Mead, 1922.

Lily Adams Beck is chiefly remembered today for her mystical visions of Eastern occultism, but she also wrote many adventure and fantasy novels under the name Louis Moresby, and published several bestsellers in the mid-1920s. This selection is representative of her best work.

"The Ninth Vibration," a long novella, tells the story of a rajah cursed by his own moral blindness, and the strange and lovely House of Beauty he built for the love of a great woman. "The Interpreter" relates the tale of a love that transcended life itself, and tells how Stephen Clifden found his destiny in the mystical mountains of Kashmir. "The Incomparable Lady" is a myth of the ancient Chinese court.

In Burma "The Hatred of the Queen" is something no woman ignores, but even mortal enemies are reconciled in times of peril. "Fire of Beauty" is a story of love and sacrifice in old India, and tells how a prophecy by the Twice-Born saved the royal line of Chitor from disgrace or extinction. "The Building of the Taj Mahal" pays homage to the undying love of a man for a woman. In "'How Great is the Glory of Kwannon!'" the goddess makes the plainest maid in the land shine with her inner beauty, and the emperor bows before them both. "The Round-Faced Beauty" had the audacity to tell the emperor the truth, and he loved her for it.

Bennet, Robert Ames. *Thyra: A Romance of the Polar Pit*. New York: Henry Holt, 1901.

Next to the impenetrable jungles of Africa and South America, the North and South Poles provided the most popular location for lost-race adventures around the turn of the century. For many years, *Thyra*, Bennet's first novel, has remained a true classic in the field, scarce and highly sought-after by collectors, both for its action-packed narrative of strange peoples and fantastic adventures and for the striking illustrations which accompany them.

A party of explorers seeking the North Pole commandeers a stray balloon that takes them to a warm, sub-surface land which has survived unchanged for millions of years. It is inhabited by a mixture of prehistoric mammals and dinosaurs, a bestial, ape-like race, and a civilization of lusty Norsemen, descendants of Vikings who had discovered the land centuries before. Using their rifles, the explorers save a young Norse girl, Thyra, and her brother, Rolf, from a giant cave bear and a group of unfriendly Norsemen who call themselves "Thorlings."

Thyra's people, the Runefolk, gratefully accept the outsiders among them, particularly huge Thord Borson, an Icelander who feels a natural kinship with this lost civilization. At the invitation of the treacherous king of the Thorlings, Hoding Grimeye, the explorers and a number of their Norse friends undertake a journey to visit his kingdom, where a gigantic idol of a prehistoric sea monster is worshipped jointly with the hideous beast men. When they learn

21

that they are to be sacrificed to the idol, the explorers destroy it, thereby precipitating a furious battle between the Norsemen and the enraged ape-men. The Norsemen are victorious, the living counterpart of the idol is faced and destroyed, and the Norsemen are freed from its terrible influence forever.

Benson, E. F. *Spook Stories*. London: Hutchinson, 1928.

E. F. Benson was the middle of three sons of a former Archbishop of Canterbury, Edward White Benson, all of whom became writers of supernatural and occult fiction interwoven with strong elements of religious influence. Probably the best-known of the three brothers (the others were A. C. Benson and Robert Hugh Benson), Edward Frederic Benson interested himself in archeology before becoming a writer, and this fascination with antiquity is noticeable in much of his work. He became one of the most distinguished practitioners of the supernatural short story, and many of his ghostly tales have become classics in the literature of weird fiction.

Spook Stories offers such horrors as a woman haunted by a recurring nightmare of a sinister face—the face of a man dead over 200 years—in "The Face"; a hideous Egyptian cat-spirit which threatens the souls of two young men in "Bagnell Terrace"; an unthinkably loathsome slug-like monster which has haunted a forest for centuries in "And No Bird Sings"; and the ghost of a murderer accidentally contacted by two mediums in "Spinach." "Reconciliation" tells of the spirit of a man who returns to haunt the house of which he was wrongfully dispossessed during his lifetime; in "A Tale of an Empty House," the invisible ghost of a lame strangler still lurks to trap the unwary; and two men are the horrified witnesses to the eternal curse on the soul of an evil man who hanged himself in "Expiation." A piano-playing ghost returns to re-enact her death and trap her murderer in "Home, Sweet Home"; and the ageless horror of "The Temple" drives men to suicide. These and other tales provide powerful examples of the ghost story at its best.

Benson, Robert Hugh. *Lord of the World*. London: Sir Isaac Pitman & Sons, 1907.

Since fundamentalist Christian beliefs were widespread at the turn of the century, it is not surprising to find numerous religious tracts disguised as fiction being published during this period. One of the better examples of these unusual hybrids is Benson's *Lord of the World*, which was published partially as a response to Edward Bellamy's *Looking Backward, 2000-1887.*

In the world of 2000 A.D., the religion of Humanitarianism is about to win the world struggle for souls over the faltering Catholic Church. The machine age has triumphed, having produced numerous air-conditioned cities (many located underground), vast highway systems, swift aircraft called "volors," a socialist government, and the widespread practice of euthanasia in state-run hospitals. Esperanto is spoken throughout the three great surviving empires of America, Europe, and the East, although some national languages still linger in isolated parts of the world.

Led by its prophet, Felsenburgh, Humanitarianism is closing in on the last desperate defenders of Rome, and as persecution of Catholics continues, the Eternal City is decimated by a fleet of Felsenburgh's volors. The last Pope, Percy Franklin, assembles his remaining cardinals in Palestine, and prays for deliverance. A great light shines down upon him from Heaven, and the Second Coming of Christ begins. "Then this world passed, and the glory of it."

Benson was the younger brother of the well-known writer, E. F. Benson.

Beresford, J. D. *The Hampdenshire Wonder*. London: Sidgwick & Jackson, 1911.

Beresford's novel is a classic treatment of the *Homo superior* theme. Victor Stott is the strange child of a famous cricket player. While still an infant he displays unusual powers of understanding and intelligence, and no man can look him in the eye without flinching. Although the infant never cries nor speaks, he seems to understand everything that goes on around him. His oversized, misshapen head causes many authorities to think him an idiot, and yet he is as far above them as they are above Neanderthal Man.

Henry Challis, the local squire, takes an interest in the Wonder, and offers him the use of his 40,000 volume library. The four-year-old boy begins his studies by reading the dictionary from cover to cover, and then the *Encyclopaedia Britannica*. When Challis asks the child what he thinks of all this accumulated knowledge, the boy attempts to tell the squire his theory of progress, but the older man cannot understand a tenth of what is said. The only person over whom the Wonder has no control is a hydrocephalous idiot who apparently sees some similarity between his huge head and that of the genius, and who consequently follows him about unmercifully. In the end, the superintelligent child is found drowned in a pond, apparently pushed there in an accident by the idiot, who just wanted to play.

The author's delineation of a superman's problems in a "normal" society is particularly well handled. This ironic novel set the tone for all later treatments of this theme.

Blackwood, Algernon. *The Centaur*. London: Macmillan, 1911.

Algernon Blackwood, one of the acknowledged masters of the supernatural short story, also produced a number of novels dealing with the psychic worlds of wonder and terror that he evokes so vividly. These novels, which have been unfairly neglected for many years, contain some of Blackwood's most beautiful and effective writing. Such a novel is *The Centaur*, of which H. P. Lovecraft, in his *Supernatural Horror in Literature* (1945) says: "Mr. Blackwood achieves...a close and palpitant approach to the inmost substance of dream, and works enormous havoc with the conventional barriers between reality and imagination."

On a steamer bound for Greece, a wild, unsettled Irish writer named Terence O'Malley befriends a strange, huge, inarticulate man and his son who are also en route to the isles, and who possess an aura of proto-human "naturalness," of kinship with pagan nature-worship, that defies analysis. O'Malley is fascinated by them, by their air of timidity combined with great, unguessable power, for they strike a chord of longing in his own soul.

Despite the concerned warnings of another friend, the ship's doctor, Heinrich Stahl, who possesses great insight and intelligence, O'Malley finds himself drawn more and more into an overwhelming compulsion to go with the big man, returning to his own kind deep in the forests and mountains of Greece. The story of O'Malley's psychic odyssey into the dim past of our planet to discover beings far older than man, still surviving in a state of cosmic bliss, truly one with Nature, is a unique and stirring experience for lovers of supernatural and occult fiction.

Blackwood, Algernon. *The Fruit Stoners: Being the Adventures of Maria Among the Fruit Stoners.* London: Grayson & Grayson, 1934.

Best known for his superb short stories of the supernatural and the occult, Algernon Blackwood also wrote several children's fantasies which are comparatively unknown, perhaps because, unlike most books with juvenile protagonists, Blackwood's were not written *for* children—but *about* them. Like *Alice in Wonderland*, which it resembles in several particulars (there is even a mad tea party!), *The Fruit Stoners* tells the story of a little girl's adventures in a strange, dreamlike world of her own hyperactive imagination, and can be appreciated on several levels.

Maria, a motherless, lonely ten-year-old, takes refuge in a fantasy world of playmates created from the prune pits arranged around her father's breakfast plate each morning— she gives each of them a name and a distinct personality: the Gentleman, the Sailor, the Ploughboy, the Soldier, etc. One evening she has just five minutes to fetch her father's slippers for him, and as she dashes up to his room, she is stopped by the tall, sinister figure of The Man Who Wound the Clocks, and forced to enter the part of the house which has been shut up and deserted for months.

Here Maria discovers a world outside of normal time, where her "Fruit Stoners" actually exist as people, just as she has imagined them. At first all is delightful—her creations love her and fawn over her, but gradually a sinister note creeps into the adventure: Maria cannot remember what she is supposed to be looking for, and her quest takes on a desperate necessity in her mind.

As she searches wildly, spurred on by the fear that this seemingly endless "five minutes" will soon be up, she discovers that she is growing up. She becomes a young woman, and is forced to pick one of the Fruit Stoners as a husband. The frantic search continues, with Time the Tiger stalking ever closer; she becomes an old woman, still looking for what she cannot remember.

Blackwood uses this "children's story" to make some of his most profound and challenging philosophic points—about time, about adolescence, about male-female relationships, and about the oftentimes inseparable worlds of fantasy and "reality."

Blackwood, Algernon. *Strange Stories.* London: William Heinemann, 1929.

Among the many volumes of novels, short stories, children's books and plays produced by Algernon Blackwood between 1906 and his death in 1951 are some of the finest short stories of the supernatural and the occult ever written. This volume brings together many of those stories that Blackwood considered his best to date, carefully selected from such earlier collections as: *The Listener* (1907), *John Silence* (1908), *Pan's Garden* (1912), and others.

"The Man Whom the Trees Loved" and "The Sea Fit" typify Blackwood's theme of man's longing for union with Nature and the non-human forces and deities existing on higher planes of consciousness. In the first story, the hero's soul unites with the spirit of the forest; in the second, a man offers himself as a sacrifice to the ancient gods of the sea. Other gods, too, are explored to chilling effect in such stories as "The Wings of Horus" and "A Descent into Egypt," in which the spell of ancient Egypt captures a man's personality and steals away his soul into past ages.

In "The Glamour of the Snow" a beautiful snow-ghost lures her willing victim into the freezing wilderness. "The Damned" is Blackwood's variation on the standard "haunted house" story: here the house is haunted by the evil presences of men damned and imprisoned by their own narrow, intolerant ideas. One of Blackwood's most famous tales, "The Willows," shows what can happen when men anger the vast and powerful forces outside humanity. "Ancient Sorceries" features the psychic detective John Silence, and deals with reincarnation, witchcraft, and the Black Mass. Many other fine stories display to excellent effect the skill of the writer whom Peter Penzoldt, in his dedication to *The Supernatural in Fiction* (1952), has called "the greatest of them all."

Boothby, Guy. *Pharos, the Egyptian: A Romance.* London: Ward, Lock, 1899.

Guy Boothby, author of the popular Dr. Nikola series, wrote many mystery and adventure novels which were extremely well received by readers on both sides of the Atlantic, and which made him one of the most widely read English writers of the late 1800s and early 1900s. Boothby introduced many elements of the occult and the supernatural into his novels, particularly in the Dr. Nikola series, but *Pharos* is perhaps his most fantastic adventure-romance.

A rising young artist, Cyril Forrester, meets a repulsive, ancient man who carries with him an aura of unguessable evil—Pharos the Egyptian. As strongly as he is repulsed by the old man, Cyril is attracted to the beautiful young Valerie de Vocxqal, Pharos's ward, who is obviously completely under his influence. Pharos visits Cyril quite suddenly one evening, demanding that the young man give him the mummy of Ptahmes, the Chief Magician of Rameses II, which Cyril's late father, a great Egyptologist, discovered and brought to England. Cyril refuses, and Pharos overpowers him and steals the mummy.

When Cyril recovers and goes to reclaim the mummy, Pharos apologizes and eventually wins him over, saying that he merely wants to replace the body of his ancestor back in the tomb from which it was wrongfully taken. Suspicious, but wanting to rescue Valerie from Pharos's clutches, Cyril accompanies the pair to Egypt, where he discovers that the old man's occult arts have trapped him in bondage just as they have Valerie, who feels they cannot escape. Slowly Cyril learns that he is merely a pawn in Pharos's terrible plan to spread a plague throughout Europe, and finally he discovers the hideous truth that Pharos is actually Ptahmes himself, alive for 3,000 years! But at the very moment of his triumph, Pharos is destroyed by the ancient gods he has defied, and Cyril and Valerie are free at last.

The Boyhood Days of Guy Fawkes; or, The Conspirators of Old London. London: "Boys of England," 1870?

No collection of supernatural fiction would be complete without an example of the oversized juvenile paperbacks so popular in England and America during the latter part of the nineteenth century. Typical of the lot is the garishly illustrated, anonymously penned *Guy Fawkes,* which makes up in verve whatever it may lack in style.

Guy is a hot-headed boy living in York Minster. His two friends, Humpy the Hunchback and Conrad Burleigh, find an old buried chest in the vault beneath York Cathedral, where Guy's father works. The dwarf begins rummaging through the casket's contents, and accidentally drops a strangely shaped bottle on the floor. Out of the broken shards of glass comes a purple light and mist, and suddenly an ancient wizard appears.

Bartholomew Clitheroe, for such is his name, draws out a magic globe, and shows Guy several scenes from his future life. The young boy is startled to see himself reflected in the glass before Queen Elizabeth I, whom he detests for her Protestant religion. Later Guy moves to London, where he is seized for making speeches against the state church. Fawkes is taken before the queen, just as the image foretold, and he denounces the monarch to her face. While waiting execution, the lad is saved with Conrad's help, and after a series of narrow escapes, the companions make their way to the castle of the adviser who had urged Guy's destruction. Powder is set in place, the fortress destroyed, and Guy, now a hunted fugitive, flees to Spain, where his exploits (as Guido Vaux) reverberate through the battlefields of Europe.

Years later, he returns to England and plots to destroy Parliament and the new King James I. But the wizard looks into his glass, and warns Guy that fate is against him. Fawkes will not be dissuaded and proceeds with his plans.

But a traitor reveals the threat to the king, and Guy is caught. The infamous outlaw finally repents his actions on the scaffold.

Bradshaw, William R. *The Goddess of Atvatabar: Being a History of the Discovery of the Interior World and Conquest of Atvatabar.* New York: J. F. Douthitt, 1892.

One of the more fanciful theories produced by the nineteenth century was the idea that the interior of the Earth is hollow, harboring a world of its own. A prime example of this fantastic notion is Bradshaw's exotic novel, *The Goddess of Atvatabar.*

Lexington White, heir to a vast fortune, sets out to explore the North Pole in a great ship of his own design. An Arctic upheaval reveals a huge vortex in the ocean which draws the explorers into an inner world lighted by a perpetually shining miniature sun. Flying men with metal wings escort the explorers to the court of the King of Atvatabar, the inner world continent lying opposite the Atlantic Ocean.

The marvels of the land are many: mechanical ostriches for cavalry, intercontinental mono-rails, airships powered by "magnicity," strange plant-animals, and mystical ceremonies by which "twin-souls" (eternally separated lovers) are dedicated to a life apart from each other in celibate service to the goddess Harikar.

Lyone, a beautiful woman thought to be the goddess incarnate, is doomed to this lonely existence until she and White fall in love. The sacrilege produces a religious civil war in which Lyone's forces and the Americans are pitted against the armies of the outraged king. A great naval battle between White's ship and the fleet of Atvatabar appears to be lost, when the tide is turned by the arrival of British and American warships, who have followed White in search of the lost expedition. The enemy fleet is captured, the king is killed, and White is the new ruler of Atvatabar, with Lyone as his consort and queen.

Bramah, Ernest. *Kai Lung Beneath the Mulberry-Tree.* London: Richards Press, 1940.

Very little is known about the life of Ernest Bramah (Smith), the reclusive author of the Kai Lung books; even the date of his birth is in dispute. Throughout his career he shunned publicity, often being evasive about himself even to his own publisher, Grant Richards. In 1942, a few months before his death, Bramah wrote to the editors of *Twentieth Century Authors* that he was "not fond of writing about myself; and only in less degree about my work. My published books are about all that I care to pass on to the reader." By far the finest of these books are the Kai Lung volumes, which have become favorites with discerning readers since the publication of the first, *The Wallet of Kai Lung*, in 1900. Bramah produced four more Kai Lung books during his lifetime, of which the present volume is the last.

Unlike the four previous books, *Kai Lung Beneath the Mulberry-Tree* was never published in the U.S. until the 1978 Arno Press reprint. Like the others, it presents a collection of marvelous tales of Old China, stories of romance and revenge and magic and mystery, told with great wit and irony by the master storyteller, Kai Lung. We are presented with the joys and tribulations of Prince Ying, Paramount Ruler of the State of Further Yin, which occurred when he exchanged clothes with a peasant to go among his people in disguise. We learn how this same Prince Ying contrived to save his land from the menaces of block printing and gunpowder. "The Story of Yin Ho, Hoa-Mi, and the Magician" tells how a mediocre student and his love, the only daughter of a dog-stealer, are mysteriously married by a magician and set on the path to higher destinies. Other stories display Bramah's best satirical wit, his impeccable and mannered style, his delightful prose, and his vision of China—a China that never was, save in the mind of the creator of Kai Lung.

Bruce, Muriel. *Mukara: A Novel*. New York: Rae D. Henkel, 1930.

Atlantis has long been one of the favorite subjects for lost-race novels; literally dozens of them were issued featuring surviving Atlantean colonies or Atlantis itself, located in such diverse realms as the Arctic and Antarctic, the jungles of Africa or South America, the Sahara Desert, and even in the Caribbean (Frank Aubrey's *A Queen of Atlantis*). Less frequently featured has been the even more ancient and mysterious lost continent of Mu, or Lemuria, thought to have been located in the Pacific Ocean millions of years ago. Drawing upon the writings of occultists and archeologists such as Madame Blavatsky, Augustus Le Plongeon, W. Scott-Elliot, and James Churchward, and suggested by notes given to her by her friend, the late Col. Percy H. Fawcett, Bruce has produced an exciting, fast-paced novel of strange adventures in a lost city of a surviving pre-Mayan culture from Mu.

In 1925 Fawcett and his son disappeared into the Amazon jungle in search of such a city in actuality, but they never returned. It was not until 1951 that it was learned that they had been murdered by Indians of the upper Xingu basin. The characters in the novel begin their expedition into the Brazilian wilds much as the Fawcetts began theirs, with Richard Kirby and his archeologist father, Freyne, a young anthropologist, and Woodcock, doctor, chemist, and physicist, comprising the main party. After harrowing adventures through jungles and desert regions, they are met by the vanguard of a lost race of whites who take them beyond a huge mountain range into a hidden valley where a beautiful city exists.

These people are the last remnant of the ancient Empire of Mu, and the advent of the strangers causes a fierce civil war between two factions and ultimately fulfills an ancient prophecy. Finally, two of the explorers stay in the hidden valley, and the other pair returns to the outside world.

Burdekin, Kay, writing as Murray Constantine. *The Devil, Poor Devil! A Novel.* London: Boriswood, 1934.

No collection of adult fantasy would be complete without a sample or two of the many novels featuring as a main character that inimitable seducer of souls, the Devil. Like most of these stories, this one is comic—yet there is a serious and almost ominous undertone, almost a combination of the styles of H. G. Wells, C. S. Lewis, and Charles Williams. Indeed, the character of the superhuman being called

"The Independent," who neither supports good nor evil, is a unique and fascinating creation worthy of Wells or Lewis.

Realizing one day that he is in danger of extinction because most men no longer believe in him, the Devil comes to earth with the Independent to see what can be done to remedy the situation. The Independent occupies the recently deceased body of Lady Delabole, a rich widow and grandmother of young Cyril Fairways, whose body the Devil takes over. The Devil has a difficult time adjusting to living in a physical body and often mistreats it before he learns better. Then he is introduced to one of the true torments of humanity: he finds himself falling in love with a beautiful young country girl, Fenella Huntly, but she is fearful of him and distant, somehow sensing his unnaturalness.

Fenella loves a modern poet, Lance Briar, who returns her affections, and the Devil's attempts to usurp this romance only cause him further torment. Finally, his frustration leads almost to madness, and to suicide and murder and the death of his host body. Fenella and Lance are now free to marry without interference, while the Devil, now without a body, realizes he has failed to revive mankind's fear of him. He now begins to shrink, getting smaller and smaller, until he is no bigger than a mouse. As he rages to the Independent, it leaves the body of Lady Delabole and with colossal laughter that shakes the sky, expands far beyond the stars.

In recent years "Murray Constantine" was revealed to be the late British feminist writer, Katharine "Kay" Burdekin.

Burrage, A. M., writing as Ex-Private X. *Someone in the Room.* London: Jarrolds Publishers, 1931.

British author Burrage, who also wrote the tales collected in *Some Ghost Stories*, here provides a chilling collection of fourteen shockers.

"The Sweeper" haunts Miss Ludgate for the unkindness that caused his death. Colin Forshaw loved the girl in "The Blue Sunbonnet," and after her death she still keeps watch over him. Raymond Hewson, an indigent reporter, decides to get his story by sitting up all night in "The Waxwork." "Through the Eyes of a Child" tells of a house haunted by the spirit of a little boy. "The Running Tide" is the name of Anstice's new boarding house, but its past history keeps the guests awake at nights. In "The Strange Case of Dolly Frewan," a young murdered girl gets revenge by possessing the killer's new lover. "The Oak Saplings" grow over two lovers' bodies, but the souls of the dead are restless in the copse. A woman returns to "The Cottage in the Wood" to find her dead husband's spirit, and some of the happiness she knew with him. "Smee" resembles hide-and-seek, but what do you do when you count fourteen heads, and you know there are only thirteen? "The Case of Mr. Ryalstone" is the strange tale of a man living two lives simultaneously. "Someone in the Room" tells of a suicide haunting the place of his death. In "Mr. Garshaw's Companion," a man is willed his wife's familiar, and can't understand why all his friends stay away. "The Shadowy Escort" is the story of a man haunted by the presence of the one he killed. "One Who Saw" tells how Crutchley has the urge to see a ghost's mutilated face, and very nearly goes mad from the shock.

Čapek, Karel, translated by Lawrence Hyde. *Krakatit*. London: Geoffrey Bles, 1925.

This satire was first published in Czechoslovakia by the author of *R.U.R.* and *War with the Newts*, and was one of the first serious treatments of the atomic bomb theme and mankind's inability to control its own weapons.

Prokop, a Czechoslovakian chemist, discovers a fantastic new explosive called "Krakatit," which is both tremendously powerful and capable of being detonated atomically by high frequency radio waves. An accidental explosion of the substance disables him, and as a result unscrupulous munitions manufacturers hear about it. Prokop awakens as a prisoner on an estate near the munitions factory, but refuses to divulge the secret of Krakatit, and after much travail manages to escape.

He is immediately grabbed by a local band of anarchists, who want to use the explosive to enslave the world. They attempt an experimental bombing, but destroy both themselves and the entire town they were attempting to terrorize. The trauma produced by this second narrow escape wipes the secret of Krakatit forever from Prokop's mind, and, at peace at last, he decides to devote the rest of his days to developing atomic power for peaceful uses.

Carew, Henry. *The Vampires of the Andes*. London: Jarrolds, 1925.

A young girl, Quitu, is left on the door of a couple in Peru, with a note saying she is the descendant of the Inca kings. On her arm is the mark of a strange bird. Her presence becomes the focus of a strange hunt, for it soon becomes clear that a bizarre cult regards her as essential to their rituals and is seeking to kidnap her.

Will Wootton, who loves the girl, mounts an expedition to the Matto-Grasso of Brazil. He discovers a cave and descends through the opening. But the passageway closes behind him, and he finds himself fighting for his life as he passes through a series of pre-arranged trials. In order to save Quitu, he must become an Initiate of the mystery surrounding the tribe of Muchacaraps, which has hidden the girl away. After crossing the abyss of flames, he comes to a chamber inhabited by a woman in the guise of a Hindu goddess. This spirit precipitates him into a bottomless hole, where he merges with the essence of a Force that reveals to him the evolution of our planet. By seeing these secrets he can give the goddess a name, and that releases him from her bondage. He is now one of the Initiates. In the underground empire, lighted by a magnetic blue radiance, men live for hundreds of years.

Deep in the central chamber of Aztlán, the fatal day approaches, when the sacred birds will fly forth and drink the blood of seven young virgins, reawakening the gigantic forms of the seven great gods of mankind. As the sun appears over the horizon, the sound of breathing is heard and the great chests stir once again. They berate mankind for his evil ways, and the weapons of destruction he has invented. "Man," they say, "must abandon the course he is pursuing," or the Day of Reckoning will destroy him. There is still time; the warning has been delivered. Quitu is saved, and the gods return to their sleep.

Carnegie, James, Ninth Earl of Southesk. *Suomiria: A Fantasy.* Edinburgh: David Douglas, 1899.

Originally issued in a limited private edition of fifty copies, this interesting fantasy is little known among histories of fantastic literature.

Sir Julian discovers strange footprints in Moneela Forest, and follows them to a tribe of hideous ape men, who have killed several little girls and captured what appears to be a female sphinx. With the help of the girl creature, Julian routs the evil troglodytes, who are dwellers in the central Earth. Suomiria comes from a neighboring country in the interior world, and she invites the man to return with her to the realm of the sphinxes. There she takes Julian to her father, the king, who grants the lovers a unique boon: Suomiria may become a woman, with an earthly soul, in return for giving up her immortality and supernatural powers. The couple are happy for a time, but Julian begins longing for his own land, and thus condemns himself to be separated from his wife forever.

The way back to England is long and hard, for the path lies directly through the land of the ape-goats, but after many travails, they return at last to Moneela Forest. Suomiria bids farewell and leaves two tokens with Julian that can be used by the bearer to call her back when the need arises. The nobleman eventually marries a girl named Rosamund, putting aside memories of his former lover. One day the pair are captured by bandits and held for ransom. They manage to escape, but are closely pursued, and when all seems lost, Julian draws out his token and calls Suomiria to his side.

The sphinx-girl destroys his enemies, but the price that must be paid is the life of the caller or his beloved. Both Rosamund and her husband insist that the other be taken, and Suomiria, torn between the two, forfeits her own human existence in sacrifice, once again becoming a sphinx. But her transformed body is claimed by the seven elderly men who suddenly appear before them. Suomiria is taken away to dwell forever in realms of mystery beyond the ken of man.

Chambers, Robert W. *The Gay Rebellion.* New York: D. Appleton, 1913.

In this amusing treatment of the women's rights movement, Chambers satirizes the suffragettes of the early 1900s. Women everywhere have begun to rebel against masculine denial of their right to vote, and enforce their demands by boycotting their fathers, brothers, sweethearts, and husbands. Marriages and births drop sharply, and economic catastrophe seems inevitable, but the men stubbornly hold out. At the heart of the rebellion is the secret, select group of beautiful women operating the New Race University, a commune dedicated to the overthrow of male domination of the world, and to the establishment of a new, physically perfect race through the twin principles of eugenics and selective breeding.

The fanatical women kidnap a number of exceptionally handsome men, and bring them to the University to be "trained" for scientific propagation. The demand for perfect spouses spreads rapidly through America and Britain, as millions of young women militantly pursue the handsome (and terrified) young men, forcing many into unhappy, scientifically correct marriages. Riots push the revolution to the edge of success, when suddenly the natural balance of things is restored by the Revolt of the Unfit. Hordes of unattractive, love-starved spinsters begin asserting their rights to the millions of imperfect men still left unmarried.

Despite attempts by their more attractive comrades to explain the benefits of eugenic breeding, the "plain Janes," encouraged by countless balding, skinny, middle-aged, and otherwise defective men, put down the revolt, and return Woman to "her own sphere to mind her own business."

Chambers, Robert W. *The Slayer of Souls.* New York: George H. Doran, 1920.

Robert W. Chambers is principally remembered today for one book, but that book is a masterpiece in the field of supernatural fiction—*The King in Yellow* (1895). Largely influenced by the sardonic fantasies of Ambrose Bierce, Chambers's book in turn became a major influence on H. P. Lovecraft and other fantasy writers of the early 1900s.

Chambers wrote other books of fantasy and science fiction, but none have achieved the status of *King*. As a writer of dozens of historical novels and society romances, Chambers all too often intruded a light touch into his writing, which tended to spoil the mood of his fantastic fiction. This fault is apparent in his early novella, *The Maker of Moons* (1896), the title story of Chambers's third collection; in spite of this he achieves a successful blending of Oriental menace, adventure and the sinister chill of occult forces at work. This story was to anticipate the popular "Yellow Peril" novels by Sax Rohmer and others that flourished in the 1920s and '30s, and was to serve as a model for Chambers's second most popular fantasy, *The Slayer of Souls*, by far his most effective supernatural novel.

Slayer has everything: sinister Oriental villains, black magic from Central Asia, German-Bolshevik plots, secret agents, occult combat, and a strong love interest throughout. Tressa Norne, an American-born girl, has been held in bondage for years in the Temple of Erlik, an Oriental devil-god of Central Asia. She escapes to America with the knowledge that a worldwide organization of murderous black magicians composed of Yezidees and Hassani are formulating a plot to enslave the world. Through the protection and love of a secret agent, Victor Cleves, Tressa finds the courage to battle black magic attempts to kill her, emerging victorious over her attackers and finally destroying the leader of the organization.

Channing, Mark. *White Python: Adventure and Mystery in Tibet*. London: Hutchinson, 1934.

White Python was the second in a four-book series of exciting and fast-moving novels of fantastic adventure featuring British Secret Service Agent Colin Gray, V.C. Strongly influenced by the works of H. Rider Haggard and Talbot Mundy, Channing set much of his fiction in India, Asia, and Tibet, where lost races and Oriental sorcery abound. This novel is by far the most fantastic of the series, and deals with an earlier period in Gray's career than the other books.

General Dalziell of the British Foreign Office sends Gray on a mission to Tibet to expose and defeat the plans of an outlaw named Chorjieff, who intends to take over Tibet, assassinate the Dalai Lama, and proclaim himself king, thereby fulfilling an ancient prophecy. Gray joins forces with an exiled lama, Samdad Chiemba, who uses occult powers to show Gray a vision of a secret lamasery in Tibet where a huge white python is worshipped by strange, sightless troglodytes and their naked high priestess, Gynia, who has a psychic rapport with the monster.

En route to Calcutta, Gray meets Piers Bryan, called by newspapers the "World's Most Famous Air-Girl," who intends to fly solo to Peking. They develop a strong liking for each other but are forced to go their separate ways all too soon. Gray pursues his secret mission, which is fraught with peril and black magic, and he learns from a resurrected corpse that Piers's plane has crashed and that she is being held captive in the mystic valley of the Python. When Gray finally reaches the secret monastery, the snake-priestess Gynia wants to make him her consort. He refuses and is imprisoned, but escapes with Piers and kills the snake, as the entire valley is destroyed by a volcanic eruption. Gray brings his mission to a successful conclusion by exposing the renegade Chorjieff and bringing him to justice.

Chester, George Randolph. *The Jingo*. Indianapolis: Bobbs-Merrill, 1912.

Webster defines the word "jingo" as "a person who boasts of his patriotism and favors an aggressive, threatening, warlike foreign policy." The word is archaic now, having been replaced by the popular term "chauvinist," but its definition certainly fits the hero of this unusual lost-race novel by a popular novelist, short-story writer, and critic of the early 1900s. Chester was best known for a series of magazine stories about a character named "Get-Rich-Quick Wallingford," who managed to make money by means both amusing and barely legal.

The Jingo is written in the same jaunty, satirical style, and the title character, Jimmy Smith, is simultaneously the original "Ugly American," a super-patriotic ass, and a sincere, likeable and courageous leader. Jimmy is shipwrecked on the shores of an unknown island named Isola, where the remnants of an ancient Greek culture live in stark simplicity and ignorance of the outside world. Pulled from the ocean by the beautiful princess Bezzanna, Jimmy quickly recovers and falls in love with his rescuer who is the king's sister. She also loves Jimmy, but the island customs forbid her to marry a commoner; she is already betrothed to a rival prince, Onalyon, who schemes to take over the kingdom by rebellion.

Jimmy loses no time in "Americanizing" the willing Isolians: with the help of a technical manual that drifted ashore with him he instructs them in the arts of manufacturing, financial exchange, and warfare. Before long, this formerly pastoral society has telephones, telegraph, a stock market, automobiles, and many other modern marvels—including gunpowder, rifles, cannon, and even land mines! These last are instrumental in overthrowing the jealous rebel Onalyon and restoring peace to Isola, which then becomes a republic when the king adopts a constitution drafted by Jimmy. Now Jimmy and Bezzanna can marry, and the king completes the Americanization process by proclaiming the kingdom a United States territory.

Clock, Herbert, and Eric Boetzel. *The Light in the Sky.* New York: Coward-McCann, 1929.

Two authors combine forces to produce an unusual and provocative lost-race novel in *The Light in the Sky*—a blend of fantasy, science fiction and the occult.

A young Allied soldier during the height of World War I finds himself pursuing a beautiful and elusive girl whom he has seen twice (but very briefly) over a relatively short period of time. He spots her again in a café, but before he can speak to her, he is drugged and kidnapped! He awakes to find himself a captive in the lost city of Aztlan, inhabited by Aztec survivors of the Spanish conquest and located in a vast cavern beneath Mexico that extends far out under the Atlantic Ocean. The soldier is unable to learn why he has been brought to this strange world until he meets a man who claims to have been a companion of Cortez named Juan Velasquez de León! From this amazing 400-year-old man, the soldier gradually learns something about his surroundings: the Aztecs who inhabit the city are also immortal and are under the influence of the High Priest Tizoc, who controls them through the unlimited powers of light.

The soldier encounters the mysterious girl again, now identified as Tinemah, Daughter of the Sun, the offspring of Montezuma! She explains to him how Tizoc, by using the forces of light, has built up a super-scientific civilization of deathless Aztec warriors who live only for the day when they can pour forth upon the upper world and destroy it with their terrible "Eighth Ray" of light in retaliation for the Spanish destruction of their civilization in Mexico.

The soldier falls in love with the princess and befriends Tizoc. He learns that he has been kidnapped to participate in a great experiment in which Tizoc will release the soldier's soul for exploration among the stars. During the experiment Naguna, Tizoc's ambitious son, kills his father, intending to use the light to enslave the world. But he cannot control the power, and destroys the cavern world as Tinemah and the soldier escape.

Coblentz, Stanton A. *When the Birds Fly South.* Mill Valley, CA: Wings Press, 1945.

Stanton A. Coblentz is best known to the science-fiction world for a career spanning five decades in which he produced many fast-paced short stories and novels for science-fiction magazines, and at least one classic, *The Sunken World* (1949), a lost-race novel dealing with the discovery of a city of Atlantean survivors living at the bottom of the ocean. But Coblentz was also a poet, author of many volumes of poetry and poetic criticism, and editor of several poetry anthologies. He founded and edited the verse quarterly *Wings* from 1933-60.

This poetic influence is evident in *When the Birds Fly South*, his first published novel, and a beautiful and original lost-race story. Popular novelist Gertrude Atherton had this to say about the book: "Not only has this remarkable book a high fiction value but the style, rich and chromatic, is a poet's prose (*not* 'poetical prose'), and the descriptions, wild, varied, and magnificent, are unsurpassed by any I have ever read.

40

There is no doubt in my mind that *When the Birds Fly South* will survive as a classic."

Dan Prescott, the member of an American geological expedition exploring unmapped mountainous regions of Afghanistan, is separated from other members of his party high up on a mountainside, but is saved from freezing by an unknown people called the Ibandru. This tribe lives in a deep valley buried within the range. A gentle, peace-loving people, they accept Prescott among them, and he soon falls in love with a young woman, Yasma. But the Ibandru are strangely different from other men: each winter, when the birds migrate, they too disappear mysteriously until spring, and Prescott is forced to spend a hard winter alone. The following year, against her misgivings, Yasma agrees to marry Prescott, but when she tries to refrain from the migratory flight out of love for him, she dies. Heartbroken, Prescott leaves the valley to return to civilization.

Colomb, Rear-Admiral P., with J. P. Maurice, F. N. Maude, Archibald Forbes, Charles Lowe, D. Christie Murray, and F. Scudamore. *The Great War of 189-: A Forecast.* London: William Heinemann, 1893.

Prior to the First World War, the future war narrative was an exceptionally popular subgenre of fantastic literature. *The Battle of Dorking*, for example, created such a stir at the time it was published (1871) that its account of Britain invaded by the Germans was even debated in Parliament. One of the best of these fictions is *The Great War of 189-*, a serious attempt by the leading military thinkers of the day to forecast the next great European conflagration. In its scope and development it can only be compared to the unpublished efforts of such present-day think tanks as the Rand Corporation.

The next world war, say these sages of 1893, will begin with an attempted assassination of a Balkan leader, and will involve all the major European states within the month. Because of their interlocking treaties, Austria, Germany, Italy, and Turkey will square off against France, Russia, Serbia, and several of the other minor states. The Germans will fight a two-front war that will have to be won quickly—if at all. Russia, however, will prove ineffectual in a relatively short period of time, and will suffer heavy losses in Poland. The first major engagements on the western front will take place in Belgium (the only unfortified section of France's border), and the Germans will have great initial success in pushing back the French.

Eventually, the German army will bog down just short of Paris, the French will recoup, and the Germans will be driven back towards the end of the war. The entrance of Britain on one side or the other will prove decisive, because of the British control of the seas. In this imaginary war, the U.K. backs the Germans, with France and Russia the chief losers. The possibility of Britain supporting France is a clear alternative at the beginning of the conflict, however, with accidental circumstances determining the outcome. The book's technique of using correspondents' reports to carry forward the narrative is particularly effective.

Comeau, Alexander de. *Monk's Magic.* London: Methuen, 1931.

Here is a delightful Rabelaisian romp in the Middle Ages, a medieval romance of the days when black magic and superstition held the land in an iron grip, when religion was a cloak for wickedness, when witches and warlocks cast mighty spells (and some small ones), and when robber barons held sway.

Into this bewildering world Brother Dismas, a lay monk, is sent by his abbot on a quest to find the fabled Elixir of Life. He soon encounters a strange and wonderful group of characters: Neluka, the old gypsy sorceress, who gives him an amulet of power; Ibrahim bin Judah, who calls up the spirit of a dead man to help Dismas, but to no avail; bawdy, barrel-shaped Thomas Brackenridge, an incorrigible rogue but a faithful companion; and a young orphan boy named Gabriel—who turns out to be a young orphan girl named Radegonde! When Radegonde is kidnapped by a henchman of the Mad Baron of the Silver Badger, Dismas rushes off to the rescue with the aid of a hideous Hand of Glory, made from the hand of a hanged man, which can open all locks.

Inside the castle of the baron, Dismas discovers that Radegonde has already escaped on her own, but he cannot leave, for an old alchemist promises to help him further in his quest for the Elixir of Life. Adventure after adventure follows, each more bizarre than the last: Dismas goes to the Land of the Dead and converses with shades who attempt to trap him there; he then witnesses a black mass and saves Radegonde from a witches' coven by using his magic amulet.

Now aware that Radegonde is a girl, Dismas finds himself falling in love with her; further adventures lead to advice from the ghost of a hermit and a great battle against the Baron's forces, utilizing both muscle and magic. But after all those episodes Dismas fails to find the elixir and returns to the abbey for his last adventure—the raising of the Devil himself!

Cook, William Wallace. *Adrift in the Unknown; or, Queer Adventures in a Queer Realm.* New York: Street & Smith, 1925.

Part of a series of popular science-fiction novels serialized in *Argosy* at the turn of the century, this book was one of the earlier works to feature wholly non-human inhabitants of other planets.

A brilliant but eccentric scientist, Professor Quinn, entices four selfish financial tycoons onto his spaceship, and kidnaps them on a voyage to Mercury. The Professor explains to the outraged capitalists (and to the burglar who has stowed away with the intention of robbing the four) that he has discovered both an anti-gravity paint and a liquid which protects against extremes of temperature. Using his inventions to build a space craft, he has now removed the four magnates from the people they mercilessly exploit.

The ship lands on Mercury, where the explorers discover a subterranean world inhabited by small creatures who possess one eye, one ear, and four hands, and who converse by means of ingenious sound boxes. The king there demands that the travelers steal a precious stone from the neighboring realm in return for their freedom. But the professor and his party are captured by the rival monarch, who condemns them to death.

When the executioner accidentally coats himself with the anti-gravity paint, and flies into space, the king pardons the Earthmen. After learning about the riches of Earth, however, the monarch decides to transport his army in Quinn's spaceship to conquer the unsuspecting planet. Terrified by this threat, the scientist devises a desperate plan whereby the burglar and the four tycoons (now reformed) can steal the ship from the king and escape back to Earth. The ship takes off, and the invasion is prevented, but the professor is left behind to an uncertain fate.

Cook, William Wallace. *Cast Away at the Pole.* New York: Street & Smith, 1926.

Prebble and Salis are attempting to find the North Pole when a balloon sweeps overhead and drags their sleeping bags (and occupants) through the air. The balloon is piloted by Griffyn, their chief rival, and when he sees what his anchor has picked up, he cuts the rope, depositing the two intrepid explorers into a tropical land somewhere in the middle of the Arctic wastes. They are immediately surrounded by man-like creatures seven feet tall, who are covered by bunches of long, red hair; the barbarians are on the verge of spearing their captives when a white woman in a beautiful gown saves them from death.

The Princess Ylma, daughter of King Boazar III, takes them to the royal residence, where they are fitted with metal caps that immediately give them full knowledge of the language. The Polar Regions, they find, are inhabited by two different races, the Nylls, a civilized race, and the Churs, the red barbarians who serve as slaves to white men, and who also have their own country near the Pole itself. Salis gives a flask of bourbon to the king, calling it the elixir of life, and when the king demands more, he is left in a quandary.

The two explorers steal one of the Nylls' magnetic cars and escape to the land of the Churs, breaking through the wall around that country in the process. The Churs, freed from their captivity, prepare to invade a land where the "elixir," prepared in quantity by the grounded balloonist Griffyn, has stupefied the soldiers and politicians alike. But all is saved when Salis distributes the brew to the invaders, and the barbarians are forced to return to their own lands. Salis bids a fond farewell to the lovely princess, and the polar explorers return to civilization in the balloon. Cook uses gentle satire to illuminate the foibles of both European and British culture.

Coppard, A(lfred) E(dgar). *The Collected Tales of A. E. Coppard.* New York: Alfred A. Knopf, 1948.

This collection of short stories, chosen by the author himself, brings together the best tales of a writer whose work has been called "a cross between Saki and Lord Dunsany." He is able to combine pathos and quiet irony, a sense of wonder and terror, a superb feeling for character, and an often lyrical prose to create some of the most memorable, whimsical and fantastic tales in the English language. From twelve of Coppard's collections, spanning a period of almost thirty years, here are thirty-eight tales, many of which treat the supernatural in a number of different ways, from sheerest whimsy to blackest irony.

"Adam and Eve and Pinch Me," for instance, probably Coppard's best-known tale, tells of a man who suddenly finds himself in spirit form and able to see into the future in a very strange way; "The Green Drake" is an amusing fable of a man and a duck; "The Fair Young Willowy Tree" describes the odd relationship of a beautiful willow tree and an ugly telegraph pole; in "Father Raven" a well-meaning old priest makes a fatal mistake on the Day of Judgment; "Clorinda Walks in Heaven" is the story of a timid virgin who dies and meets the husbands of her previous reincarnations in Heaven; and "Ahoy, Sailor Boy!" describes the meeting of a sailor with a very unusual young lady in what has been called "one of the most astonishing ghost stories to come from a contemporary writer."

Of his supernatural tales, Coppard has written:

> I have not the slightest belief in the supernatural. If I should ever see a ghost I should know it was time for me to consult an oculist.... All the same I have written a few ghost stories and quite a number of fantastic

tales.... And I like doing this...for with its enchanting aid a writer can ignore problems of time and tide...and abandon himself to singular freedoms on the aery winds of the Never-was.

Corelli, Marie. *The Strange Visitation of Josiah McNason: A Christmas Ghost Story.* London: George Newnes, 1904.

In a story reminiscent of Dickens's *A Christmas Carol*, Josiah McNason is the villainous millionaire, a hard-hearted businessman who humbugs with the best of them. But McNason is jolted out of his complacency by the arrival on Christmas Eve of a horrible little goblin, whose yellow body looks like a large spider in red tights. The goblin is the spirit of an ex-tightwad who now resides in hell, and he warns McNason that the old man is headed in the same direction. To emphasize his point, the creature suddenly sprouts a pair of wings and grabs the millionaire by his neck. They join a bizarre church service peopled entirely by goblins.

The preacher, Goblin "Firebrand," tells his audience that in their earthly lives they were all good churchgoers, but their charity was self-serving, meant only to advance their names and positions before the public eye. Then he points to McNason, welcoming him as a future addition to their clan. A second hurried flight brings the old scrooge to another scene, where he views the beautiful girl he once jilted because she had no money. A third flight, and he sees a former employee, now crippled and desperately in need of an operation; a few hundred pounds would cure the man's ailment, but McNason had refused to give more than five. Another journey carries the miser two thousand years into the future, where he finds London reduced to fields where shepherds tend their flocks; the memories of all his enterprises have completely faded away. Finally, he sees his own deathbed, with the doctors milking his estate for everything they can get.

Shaken to the core, McNason is returned home, determined to begin life anew while he has the chance. He immediately writes out a check for the stricken employee and dispatches it by special messenger. Carolers singing outside his door bring tidings of Christmas Day, and Josiah McNason feels his heart stir for the first time in a great many years.

Cousin de Grainville, Jean-Baptiste François Xavier. *The Last Man; or, Omegarus and Syderia: A Romance in Futurity*. London: R. Dutton, 1806.

While traveling in Syria, a young man finds a cave, wherein a spirit appears before his eyes. "I am the celestial Spirit to whom eternal futurity is known. All events are to me as if they were passed. Here Time is loaded with chains, and his empire destroyed. In me behold the father of prescience and dreams...I have conducted thy steps to this cavern, for the particular purpose of raising before thee the veil which conceals dark futurity from man, and to make thee a spectator of the scenes that will terminate the destinies of the universe."

The last days of man are restored on the side of a magical mirror. The last inhabitants of the universe are Omegarus, a young, handsome man, and his beautiful consort, Syderia. His father was king of Europe, but gradually the land became depopulated as fewer and fewer children were born. After his parents' death, a vision told him of the other sole survivor, Syderia; they represent the last hope of mankind. But men have exhausted their time on earth, and the earth itself is doomed to destruction. Syderia falls beneath the hand of Death, who is striding rapidly forward to claim his own. And Omegarus is left, the last mortal on earth—but not for long.

Cowan, Frank. *Revi-Lona: A Romance of Love in a Marvelous Land*. Greensburg, PA: Tribune Press, 188_?

Privately printed by the author in the late 1800s, *Revi-Lona* is probably the most unusual lost-race novel ever written. Although amusingly mild by today's standards, by the Victorian attitudes toward sex prevalent in the last century, this book must have been damned as the vilest pornography! This opinion, combined with an undoubtedly small press run, probably accounts for the extreme scarcity of this novel today, and also for the fact that it is unknown to all but the most knowledgeable dealers and collectors. Clumsily written, the novel nevertheless demonstrates a remarkably ingenious imagination, creating a fascinating lost land near the South Pole inhabited by a highly intelligent white-skinned race of beautiful Amazonian women who rule over small, effeminate males.

These Amazons have a well-developed society, a kind of benevolent communism, long on technological achievements, but without a soul. Colossal, elaborate buildings are built without the use of metal tools, and love and kinship are unknown. Into this paradise of love-starved women comes Anson Oliver, the only survivor of a doomed whaler, drifting in Polar seas for months. The inevitable occurs as Oliver, the only handsome, masculine male the women of Revi-Lona have ever seen, cuts a swath through the ruling women which results in a huge population boom!

At first, he appears as a hero to the populace, and the "civilized" innovations he introduces into their lives are beneficial and welcome; but gradually a darker note creeps into the picture as disease, alcohol, and civil strife begin to upset the carefully controlled ecology of Revi-Lona. Finally, horrified at what he has inadvertently brought upon this wonderful land and its colorful people, he finds himself the sole survivor of a natural volcanic cataclysm which completes the total destruction he innocently began.

Crawford, F. Marion. *With the Immortals*. London: Macmillan, 1888, 2 vols.

F. Marion Crawford's reputation as a writer of weird fiction rests primarily with his fine short stories, several of which—"The Upper Berth" and "The Dead Smile"—have become classics of horror literature. However, a number of his many popular novels contain threads of both the supernatural and of mysticism. Primarily historical romances, they reflect his knowledge and love of Italy and his amazing command of over fifteen languages. Crawford traveled extensively and became familiar with Oriental cultures and mystical beliefs. His novel *Khaled* (1891) is an Arabian fantasy, while *Zoroaster* (1885) is an historical romance based on the life of the great Persian prophet.

With the Immortals remains, however, his most unusual work, not really a novel at all in the true sense, but a series of philosophical and religious dialogues strung onto a bizarre supernatural storyline. Augustus Chard, his wife, sister, and mother-in-law are vacationing on the Mediterranean in an Italian villa, and to pass the time, Augustus engages in some elaborate and advanced experiments with electricity.

The results of these experiments are spectacular: a huge electrical storm which almost annihilates the entire party, and even stranger, the materialization of the spirits of many famous men from the past. Heinrich Heine, Chopin, da Vinci, Samuel Johnson, Julius Caesar, Pascal, and many others discuss art, philosophy, literature, politics, religion, and other subjects with the bewildered but delighted vacationers. Crawford's amazing erudition and versatility is displayed in a fascinating and unusual fashion before the shades fade away into the spirit world.

Cummings, Ray. *The Man Who Mastered Time.* Chicago: A. C. McClurg, 1929.

Loto Rogers and his father accidentally invent a device which can see into the future. In the grim world of the year 28,204, snow and ice have taken over much of the Earth, and few men survive. Loto is determined to discover a means of visiting the future, for he has seen within his projector a beautiful girl held captive against her will, and he vows to rescue her from her abductors. With funding from a scientific society he builds a combination helicopter/time machine, and takes off on his voyage through time.

After many narrow escapes, Rogers saves the girl Azeela from her kidnapper, Toroh, and returns her to her homeland, an island off the south coast of the U.S. The Anglese, as they call themselves, are the last vestiges of civilization in the world, everything else having succumbed to the cold or disease. Only the tropical region can now support life. Toroh, a renegade scientist determined to overthrow the government, is building an army of barbarian tribesmen from the mainland, and will invade shortly. Loto sends a message back to the twentieth century, requesting help from his father.

The elder Rogers builds a second craft from the plans of the first, and with his son's friend George joins Loto in the future. But Toroh steals one of the planes, and returns to the past to find more potent weapons. Armed with these superior devices, he sends his army in two great waves towards separate parts of the island. Loto and George have organized all airborne battalions of Anglese to attack the invading barges, and one force is turned back with heavy losses on both sides. But the second force lands unopposed, and all seems lost until Azeela's father, a noted scientist, destroys the barbarians by revitalizing a dormant volcano. A democracy is established by the survivors, and the three scientists, with two new brides from the future, return to their New York home.

Dalton, James, as anonymous author. *The Gentleman in Black.* London: William Kidd, 1831.

Louis Desonges needs money, and the devil is happy to oblige. The terms are very reasonable: Desonges must agree to sin for a single second during the first year, two the second, with the figure doubling each successive annum, all previous sins to be counted against the total sum. In return, Louis will have health, wealth, and long life.

The young man agrees, and signs his name to the document. At about the same time, Louis's English friend, Charles Maxwell, has come to similar straits, having squandered his inheritance, and the gentleman in black offers his services once again, with the same results. The two gadabouts tour Europe together, and manage to thoroughly debauch themselves in a dozen different countries. But both weary of this empty kind of life, and finally settle down with beautiful wives, raise families, and begin to take an interest in business, with some success.

Twenty-eight years later, Maxwell suddenly realizes that his annual tribute has increased substantially, to an annual demand of 2,330 days of sin. He consults his father's old solicitor, Bagsby, for advice in the matter. The ancient lawyer asks for samples of the devil's cash, and has it analyzed: when he finds the notes to be forgeries, Bagsby has the devil arrested. All sums paid via bank notes are discounted from the total amount due, still leaving, however, a considerable amount of cash paid to Maxwell in gold. The irritated demon refuses to accept a check for the rest until the solicitor threatens to throw the entire case into the courts, and not even Satan himself can abide the thought of all those years of lawsuits: he immediately accepts the cash, and provides a receipt in full of all demands.

Louis's case is more demanding and complicated, and Maxwell sends Bagsby to his friend's aid. The old lawyer teams with a flinty Jesuit, and the two convince the fiend to amend the deed: half the monies paid, half the sins remitted, with a grace period of fourteen years. When Satan points out that Desonges will not survive the term, he realizes that he has been tricked again, and vows to seek Bagsby's counsel in the future to avoid such disappointments with other prospective customers.

de la Mare, Walter. *The Return.* London: Edward Arnold, 1910.

"*The Return* was written as a 'pot-boiler,' a 'shocker,' and designed to earn money for its author; instead it brought him the Polignac Prize." So writes Edward Wagenknecht in a preface in his anthology, *Six Novels of the Supernatural.* Walter de la Mare is thought by many critics to be one of the finest British writers who ever lived; certainly he has no peer as a children's poet, and his short stories of the supernatural will endure as long as there is interest in the field. His long and varied career as poet, writer of delightful wonder tales for children, novelist, short story writer, and anthologist has given us some of the most sensitive and imaginative writing in the English language. This early "shocker" was first published in 1910, then revised and reissued in 1922, but it remains a landmark in the history of supernatural fiction, primarily for its sense of reality about the characters, both major and minor, as they struggle to understand forces beyond their comprehension. H. P. Lovecraft has said of de la Mare that his writing

...bear(s) traces of a strange vision reaching deeply into veiled spheres of beauty and terrible and forbidden dimensions of being. In the novel *The Return* we see the soul of a dead man reach out of its grave of two centuries and fasten itself upon the flesh of the living, so that even the face of the victim becomes that which had long ago returned to dust.

Arthur Lawford, middle-aged father and husband, sickly, dull and unassertive, wanders into a graveyard and is possessed by the spirit of Nicholas de Sabathier, an eighteenth-century French rogue and adventurer who finally committed suicide. From then on, Lawford and his family and friends are faced with a horrifying, incredible situation; and ultimately, Arthur finds that he alone must face the thing that has possessed his body, mind, and soul.

De Mille, James, as anonymous author. *A Strange Manuscript Found in a Copper Cylinder*. New York: Harper & Bros., 1888.

A common device used to bridge the mundane and fantasy worlds in early imaginative literature was the lost narrative discovered in the opening chapters. De Mille's anonymous novel is typical of the lot.

A manuscript is found floating in a copper cylinder by sailors, and is read aloud by its discoverers. The story tells of one Adam More, shipwrecked in southern latitudes in 1843, and left to drift in an open boat with his companion, Agnew. Their first stop is an island inhabited by black cannibals, who entice the men on shore and dine on Agnew. More barely escapes, and is drawn by currents southward across the sea towards a vast mountain range. The boat plunges through a dark tunnel beneath the peaks, and emerges in a calm inland sea surrounded by green, fertile lands, although this area should be, by More's best calculations, in the Polar region. Upon landing, he finds a strange race very much resembling Arabs. They take him to their underground city, where he is taught a language similar to Arabic by the beautiful Almah, and discovers that the cultural and moral values of this peculiar race are weirdly inverted.

The pseudo-Arabs see better in the dark than in daylight. They seek poverty, giving their possessions to whomever will take them; they long for death as the highest blessing of their lives; and, although peaceful, they practice human sacrifice and cannibalism on hundreds of willing victims. Adam and Almah fall in love, and find that they are destined to be given the honor of dying for her people. At the last moment, More kills several of the populace with his rifle, and the multitudes, awe-stricken, fall down and worship him as a god who can bring the greatest good—death—instantly.

The Arctic and Antarctic regions were frequently employed as settings for lost-race novels during the last half of the nineteenth century, and De Mille's narrative is one of the more colorful examples of this genre.

Dixon, Thomas. *The Fall of a Nation: A Sequel to The Birth of a Nation*. New York: D. Appleton, 1916.

This interesting example of the "America-invaded" theme was written by the author of *The Clansman*, which was later made by D. W. Griffith into the well-known classic silent film, *The Birth of a Nation*.

Virginia Holland is the young and beautiful champion of a strong women's rights movement which advocates peace and universal brotherhood through complete disarmament. She has many supporters, including Charles Waldron, a cold, domineering multi-millionaire. Her primary opponent, crusading relentlessly for military preparation against possible invasion, is Congressman Henry Vassar. Virginia is attracted to Vassar, and tries to sway him to her cause; but, although he soon falls in love with her, Vassar's principles are unshaken, and the pair remain political enemies. Then, unable to defeat the entrenched might of Germany, the Allies agree to an armistice in 1916, and an international peace conference is convened at The Hague. With the war over, American optimism is high, and prosperity reigns. Virginia's peace program is overwhelmingly approved, and Vassar's bill defeated.

A few months later, New York is suddenly bombed without warning by European planes. Enemy troops come out of hiding and take over the city, cutting all communications, and Waldron, who has betrayed his country to the imperialists, proclaims himself Governor General of the Provinces of North America. Unprepared and almost totally defenseless, the country is soon crushed by the invading Europeans led by Germany. But Vassar and Virginia organize a strong underground movement, and after much travail kill Waldron, throwing out the foreigners. America is saved and has learned her lesson, but only at the cost of billions of dollars and millions of lives. Dixon's novel was intended to help force America's participation in World War I, an event which indeed occurred just a year later.

Doughty, Francis Worcester. *Mirrikh; or, A Woman from Mars: A Tale of Occult Adventure.* New York: Burleigh & Johnstone Co., 1892.

George Wylde is traveling in Cambodia when he meets a strange man with a multi-colored face, yellow on top, black on the bottom. Wylde and Mirrikh, as he calls himself, are pursued by a mob into an alley, where the strange fellow literally dissolves into the ground, leaving behind his parcel. Wylde's friends examine the contents of the bag, and discover that the stranger is a visitor from Mars, who has arrived on this world via astral projection. Suddenly, Mirrikh appears in their midst, and offers to take any one of them back with him to Mars. The way station for interplanetary travel is Psam-dagong, a monastery hidden deep in forbidden Tibet, and it is there that the explorers must go. The monks maintain a body bank to provide receptacles for the incoming shades, and outgoing travel is facilitated by a rare gas that preserves the earth-bound bodies of the voyagers indefinitely without tissue damage, and allows their spirits to roam free.

George's friend Maurice De Veber and Mirrikh leave on their journey to the red planet, and shortly thereafter floods cause a dam above the fortress to burst, threatening all with inundation. Quickly the lamas make George and his companions inhale the gas, and then inject the inert bodies of the men into an underground escape tube. After wandering the aether, George's spirit finally returns to his body, and he awakens deep inside a dark cavern beneath the mountainside. With the help of Mirrikh's projection, Maurice is also restored to his body, and his Martian wife installed in the body of a dying girl. The explorers are provided with a new pass to leave the country, and return to civilization, awed by the marvels they have seen.

Dunn, J. Allan. *The Flower of Fate.* London: C. Arthur Pearson, 1928.

Dick Thorne is approached by the aged Chinaman, Chin Yu Wei, who has a strange errand for the westerner: in return for receiving a vast copra estate, Thorne must steal a statue from the house of a wealthy Japanese art collector, which he had in turn stolen from Chin Yu Wei's family during the upheavals of the Boxer Rebellion. Thorne agrees to accept the challenge, and manages to sneak his way into the collector's vault. As he grabs the statue, the millionaire returns, and he drops it to the floor, splitting it open: inside is a rolled scroll. Snatching up the scroll, he makes his escape, after close pursuit by the Japanese gendarmes.

Chin explains that the scroll tells the location of an undiscovered island in the South Pacific where a unique flower grows, guarded by a priesthood thousands of years old. This blossom contains the secrets of good and evil: no man may lie after smelling its fragrance. He will use the flower to reshape the world. Chin, Thorne, and the Chinaman's western ward, Gloria, set sail in the Oriental's yacht.

After weeks of pushing south, they finally sight the volcanic isle not far from where it is marked on the ancient chart. The priests have been waiting for them, in fulfillment of the old prophecy. But Chin's brother, Shih-k'ai, has been following in his own craft, trying to steal the secret from his sibling. In a dramatic confrontation, Chin kills his brother to save Dick's life. But before they can find the remnants of the flowers, the volcano erupts, and the island begins falling apart. They just manage to reach their vessel before the crater explodes and the land sinks beneath the waves. Chin is overwhelmed with self-reproach and dies on the return voyage; and Dick inherits his copra estate, settling down with Gloria Richardson, foster daughter of an ancient race.

Eddison, E. R. *Styrbiorn the Strong.* London: Jonathan Cape, 1926.

Eddison is best known today as the author of *The Worm Ouroboros*, considered by some to be the greatest single novel of heroic fantasy ever written. A genial, cultured British civil servant, Eddison also wrote three other novels, known as the Zimiamvian Trilogy, only loosely connected to *Worm*, and although recently reprinted, they are not up to the standards of his magnum opus.

Eddison was greatly influenced by the writing and translations of Icelandic sagas of William Morris, and in 1926 essayed one of his own. The result was an historical Viking novel called *Styrbiorn the Strong*, based on brief passages from such sources as the *Eyrbyggja Saga* and Snorri's *Heimskringla*, translated by William Morris and Eirikr Magnfisson, and on a record in the *Lives of the Kings* (1830) entitled *Styrbjarnar Sviakappa*.

Styrbiorn has been completely overlooked in the recent revival of interest in Eddison, probably because it has been considered only history, but this obscurity is undeserved—hints of the supernatural do occur during the story in the form of prescient dreams; and the final chapter, "Valhalla," when Styrbiorn and the other heroes are taken up into the arms of Odin All-Father and transported by beautiful Valkyries into paradise, features some of the finest fantasy writing in the English language.

The story tells of young Styrbiorn, exiled from Upsala by his uncle, King Eric, and of his battles and deeds of valor, his betrayal by his uncle's wife, his allegiance with the fierce Jomsburg Viking Palnatoki and his men, and his final great battle to overthrow Eric and claim his inheritance as King of Sweden. *Styrbiorn the Strong* is a book that will thrill and delight any admirer of E. R. Eddison and of heroic fantasy.

Edwards, Gawain. *The Earth-Tube*. New York: D. Appleton, 1929.

One of the best science-fiction novels of the 1920s, this book combines the twin themes of advanced scientific invention and the "Yellow Peril."

The world of the future is shaken by an abnormal number of earthquakes, and a courageous young scientist, King Henderson, advances the theory that a tunnel is being built through the Earth from Asia to South America. Government officials refuse to credit his "crackpot" ideas, until the terminus of the tunnel is uncovered near Buenos Aires. The scientists of the Asian Empire have developed a number of terrible war machines, and have constructed a tube made of indestructible metal through the center of the world. A city made of this same metal has now been erected on a man-made island near the end of the tunnel.

From this city issues forth an apparently endless horde of invincible tanks, wielding gas guns and death rays. The tanks cannot be stopped by Western technology, and will soon conquer the entire Western Hemisphere unless something can be done. Henderson undertakes a desperate mission. Secretly entering the Asian fortress, he rides the tube through the Earth to the heart of the Asian Empire, hoping to find some way of destroying the metal. But the scientist is captured by the emperor and condemned to death. At the last moment, Diane, a white girl held captive in the emperor's harem, helps him escape, and they find the one weakness of the seemingly impervious super-metal. At great peril, the pair manages to travel back through the tube to America, where the Western forces are told that liquid air is all they need to dissolve the threat. The Asiatic machines are soon destroyed, and the yellow hordes flee in defeat.

England, George Allan. *The Golden Blight*. New York: H. K. Fly, 1916.

This novel is a good example of a political commentary disguised as fiction. Pro- and anti-socialist tracts proliferated during the first two decades of the twentieth century, and England's book was intended to support the socialist movement.

John Storm has invented a device that can destroy gold anywhere in the world by radioactive means. Storm tells the richest man in the world, Van Horne Murchison, that all the gold in the world will be eliminated unless Murchison and his fellow capitalists agree to end war. The billionaire laughs at the poor inventor, until all the gold in Manhattan suddenly turns to dust, and the resulting riots nearly destroy the business district. The great merchants and businessmen decide to end this threat to their profits by having Storm secretly murdered, despite the scientist's warning that the destruction of gold will continue automatically even after his death. But the assassins fail, and the circles of radiation continue to widen with each passing day.

Only one person, Graf Braunschweig, has the answer: he, the richest Jew in Europe, will personally redeem every bit of gold dust in the world for silver bullion, and the world system of business will yet be preserved. Graf has guessed the truth, that the gold will eventually return to its original form when the destructive radiation is exhausted. In his ultimate triumph of cornering the world's gold market, Braunschweig takes his fellow capitalists into his vaults in Washington, and gloats as the gold starts to reform. But the dust occupies less space than the revived metal, and the trapped businessmen suddenly find themselves swept up and immolated by molten gold. With the gold standard dead forever, the peoples of the world overthrow their masters, and finally inherit the earth they have worked so hard to gain.

Erckmann-Chatrian, pseud. of Émile Erckmann and Alexandre Chatrian. *The Man-Wolf and Other Tales.* London: Ward, Lock & Tyler, 1876.

This classic tale of lycanthropy and a hereditary curse was first published in France. Doctor Fritz is invited by his foster father, Gideon Sperver, to return with him to Castle Nideck, where the count lies ill with a strange malady. Once each year near the Christmas season, an old woman appears in the Black Forest, and as she draws ever nearer to the great fortress, the old count is consumed with mad fits and ravings. Somehow, he can always sense her unseen presence, and when "The Black Death," as the old hag is called, leaves the vicinity after two or three weeks, he always seems to recover his normal health within a short period of time.

But this year the attacks have been worse than usual, and Odile, the count's comely daughter, fears for his life. Fritz examines the nobleman, but his remedies seem to have no effect. As Fritz and Gideon are discussing the situation, the howl of a wolf brings them running to the count's room, where they find the old man crouching on all fours, his arms bent forward, eyes glaring. From the dark woods comes the answering howl of a she-wolf. Later that night the doctor wakes from his sleep to see the old hag leading Count Yeri-Hans out of the castle, and silently he follows the pair into the mountains.

At the edge of a precipice, the man and woman go through the motions of casting an invisible sack over the edge of the cliff, and then the count quietly returns to his home. The next day, Fritz and Gideon pursue the witch to her den, but she dies before they can get her to confess. It remains for Knapwurst, the Castle dwarf and historian, to elucidate the story of the Counts Nideck. The first of the line, Hugh the Wolf, murdered his first wife, and was cursed together with all of his descendents for a thousand years. When the image of his murdered countess reappears, says the dwarf, then will the she-wolf finally be silent.

Leading them all down into a sealed room, he draws the curtains back from a portrait of Hugh's dead wife, and they gaze with astonishment on the features of Odile, Yeri-Hans's daughter. The curse is lifted and Nideck saved. Other stories in this collection include: "Myrtle," "Uncle Christian's Inheritance," "The Bear-Baiting," "The Scape-goat," and "A Night in the Woods."

Ewers, Hanns Heinz, translated by S. Guy Endore. *Alraune*. New York: John Day, 1929.

The mantle of German fantastic fiction in this century was inherited by Hanns Heinz Ewers, who added to the romantic supernaturalism of Tieck, Hoffmann, and Meinhold a fascination with morbid psychology gleaned from Freud and Poe, and a daring feel for decadence, sensuality, and evil found in the works of Baudelaire and Huysmans. The result was a series of weird and horrifying novels, studies in supernatural evil blended with human lust and cruelty.

Originally published in Germany in 1911, *Alraune* was Ewers's second novel, and was first translated into English in 1929 by Guy Endore, himself the author of the classic *Werewolf of Paris* (1933). Alraune is a beautiful, soulless woman, deliberately created as a human mandrake by an evil experiment in artificial insemination—her mother a prostitute, her father a rapist-murderer executed on the guillotine. Her mother dies in agony soon after Alraune's birth, as does the doctor who delivers her, only the first two of many victims to perish at her whim.

As Alraune grows up, her cunning cruelty causes untold misery among her friends and teachers; her influence is hypnotic and her attitude cold and amoral. When she reaches womanhood, lover after lover falls under her sensual, sadistic spell—and each dies or is ruined utterly. Finally, Frank Braun, Alraune's "cousin" and the man who originally suggested the idea of her conception, returns home and they become lovers. Against his will, Frank feels himself pulled down towards degradation and death, but now Alraune finds herself awakening for the first time to the delights and torments of love. Realizing at last what she is and fearing that she may kill Frank like all the others, Alraune finally ends her own life.

Farrère, Claude, translated by Elisabeth Abbott. *Useless Hands* (*Les condamnés à mort*). New York: E. P. Dutton, 1926.

James Fergus MacHead Vohr, the "Wheat King" and head of the American Siturgic Monopoly, is dictator of the Western Hemisphere in the year 199-. Hundreds of thousands of workers toil daily in Vohr's "Blocks," his city of steel skyscrapers and neat, identical apartments. Although the workers have all the material comforts they need, the monotony of their work, and the complete regulation of their lives, tend to dehumanize them into unthinking automatons. Civilization is wholly dependent on the Machine, all creativity is stifled, and the worker is merely another cog in the great mechanism of production.

Suddenly the workers' latent hostilities explode in an orgy of machine destruction. Feeling this insurrection must be put down for the good of civilization, Vohr turns his terrible disintegrating ray on 400,000 men, women, and children, and kills them all in seconds. However, Vohr learns shortly thereafter that his daughter was among the innocent victims of the ray, and he abdicates his position in sorrow. But the rule of the Machine continues; as machines become more automatic, "useless" human hands will become unnecessary and may therefore be eliminated.

First published in France, this novel by Farrère (the pseudonym of Charles Bargone) was among the first to warn of the dangers attending civilization's dependence on the Machine to the detriment of human dignity and freedom.

Fawcett, E. Douglas. *Hartmann the Anarchist; or, The Doom of the Great City.* London: Edward Arnold, 1893.

The enormous popularity of Jules Verne's novels in the late 1800s spurred a great number of imitations. *Hartmann the Anarchist,* one of the better of these Verne-inspired romances, is patterned closely after the Frenchman's *Robur the Conqueror,* although Fawcett's novel contains more elements of violence and destruction than are commonly found in Verne.

A young Socialist reformer named Stanley is kidnapped by Rudolf Hartmann, who is determined to use the power of his unique airship to overthrow the governments of Europe and England, and to replace civilization with anarchy. Hartmann's fabulous craft, the *Attila,* is powered by an anti-gravity metal, and bears many other similarities to Robur's airship *Albatross.* Hartmann tries convincing Stanley to join his crew, but the socialist refuses. After a series of exciting aerial adventures, including the cold-blooded destruction of a battleship, Stanley manages to escape the anarchist by parachuting to earth during the nightmarish bombardment of London with explosives and liquid fire. All efforts to defend the city prove futile, and it appears that London is finally doomed.

But Stanley learns that Hartmann's mother was among the victims of the attack, and sends a message to the anarchist telling him the results of his crimes. Unable to face life after the death of the only person he loved, Hartmann destroys the *Attila* in a massive explosion, killing both himself and his crew. Anarchism and political terrorism were strong social movements at the time of this book's publication, and frequent themes in the SF and future-war publications of the late nineteenth century.

Fielding, Henry. *A Journey from This World to the Next.* London: Harrison & Co., 1783.

Fielding intended this novel as a satire of British society and the mores of his time. The author says he obtained this story from a stationer to whom it was given by a gentleman in exchange for nine months' rent. Only fragments of the original remain, the rest having been sold for waste before they could be saved.

The narrative begins: "On the first of December, 1741, I departed this life, at my lodgings in Cheapside." By the laws of Fate, the narrator must wait until his body is cold before he can find his way out of the corpse through his nostrils. Now in spirit form, he perceives a young man nearby with wings on his heels: Mercury, it seems, has been assigned the task of collecting the souls of the newly dead for their voyage to the Other World. The god escorts his newest arrival to the coach stop in Warwick Lane, where the narrator meets six other spirits waiting for their ride. The stage sets off, and the travelers finally stop at an inn in the City of Diseases, where they are obliged by the laws of the underworld to pay their respects to the particular Lady who assisted them in throwing off their earthly shackles.

Resuming their journey, they come to the stately Palace of Death, and are presented to His Most Mortal Majesty, whose courtiers are all ex-sovereigns in their own right. Nearby is the River Cocytus, which they cross by boat, and as they continue forward on foot, they meet the souls of those unfortunate individuals who are being sent back to Earth for another round of existence. Those who fail to be passed by the great judge Minos for entry either into Elysium or the depths must take their chances on a monstrous Wheel of Fortune, where they are allotted new lives by chance. Each is given a slip detailing his new existence, with its usual mixture of good and ill, and then the soul is plunged into the river of forgetfulness before being allowed to enter a new human body. But the narrator is judged by Minos to be fit for the blessed plains, and so he enters Elysium, where he meets the spirits of many famous persons and hears their life stories.

Flammarion, Camille. *Omega: The Last Days of the World*. New York: Cosmopolitan Publishing Co., 1894.

A giant comet approaches the Earth of the twenty-fifth century, and men everywhere tremble at the possibility of the world's destruction. The scientists are divided, some saying the comet will poison the atmosphere, and others predicting ten million more years of life for human civilization. The Martians, by means of radio-transmitted symbols, indicate the head of the comet will strike somewhere in Italy, and urge evacuation from that region. During a tense period of waiting, the air begins to grow drier and hotter, and many of the old and infirm succumb to respiratory ailments.

Finally the danger passes, and mankind buries its many casualties. But man himself remains and flourishes, building even loftier civilizations than before. Gradually, the continents are leveled off by wind and wave; mountains disappear, and the seas rise. War is abolished when the women of the world refuse to marry any man who has borne arms, and a world state is finally formed. At the apogee of existence, men communicate psychically with Mars and Venus, and are able to perform unimaginable marvels with science and technology.

Slowly, however, water is absorbed into the Earth's interior, never to return, and the world begins to grow progressively colder and drier. And in the end, ten million years hence, what is left of man is concentrated at two spots on the equator in the slight valleys marking the remnants of the world's last oceans. The last man and woman, finding nowhere to go, nothing but the cold, and no water, die in each other's arms as the spirit of the Pharaoh Cheops comforts them. This panoramic novel of the human race is the direct literary ancestor of Olaf Stapledon's *Last and First Men*, and is justifiably famous on its own merits.

Fleckenstein, Alfred C. *The Prince of Gravas: A Story of the Past.* Philadelphia: G. W. Jacobs, 1898.

The Baron von ___, one of Germany's leading scholars, comes into the possession of a gigantic mummy, from a time and civilization unknown. He decides to use the new science of psychometry to relive the man's life. As he concentrates his mental powers on the body lying before him, the present fades away, and he is suddenly standing in the midst of a great multitude. He realizes that his father, the Prince of Gravas, has died, and he is attending the funeral service; then his brother, the hated sibling who had turned his father unjustly against him, is proclaimed the new prince by the young queen, and Almar must leave once again.

But Queen Hosyra has a mission for the young lord, to penetrate the castle of his brother, and learn Prince Gregar's plans for subverting the kingdom. The queen is the last of her line, and the man who marries her becomes king; the two strong princes of the land, Gravas and Alcazeda, have joined forces to steal away the throne, after which one will marry the queen. Almar overhears his brother plotting against the queen, but is seen as he rides away. The die is cast: both princes gather their forces to march on the capital.

Almar is made Duke and commander of the queen's forces; he meets the army of his brother in a narrow mountain pass, and has almost defeated him when the queen, faint of heart, forces a withdrawal. Gregar's forces combine with Alcazeda's, and the two men bear down on the city, bottling up the queen's men. A long siege ensues, in which the defenders are plagued by starvation and internal unrest. Finally, Almar is forced to sally forth, with disastrous results. The queen determines to betray her lover into the enemy's hands and end the siege.

But the duke, learning of Hosyra's treachery, leaves the city secretly during the night. He manages to sneak his way into Gregar's camp, but is surrounded; again he has been betrayed. As Gregar gathers the fagots for a funeral pyre of living agony, Almar casts his sword like a giant spear, piercing his brother's side. The new Prince of Gravas meets the queen at their appointed rendezvous; Hosyra throws back his hood, ready to kiss her new lover, and shrieks her fear and agony. Almar, the Prince of Gravas, is avenged!

Fyne, Neal, pseud. *The Land of the Living Dead: A Narration of the Perilous Sojourn Therein of George Cowper, Mariner, in the Year 1835.* London: Henry J. Drane, 1897.

Three seamen survive the wreck of the schooner *Witch-hazel:* George Cowper, the second mate, an old sailor named Williams, and an apprentice, Edward Miles. The trio drift in an open boat until they come across another vessel filled with dead men. While they examine the bodies, a third boat approaches, with twenty-four rowers and a small group of officials standing near the mast. The newcomers proclaim their leader to be the mighty Justin, Lord of the Land of the Living Dead, who has "refrained from willing" that the fugitives should live. For no man can swear allegiance to this great lord and then seek to leave his sway.

The survivors are taken to the Land, located on a forgotten island. Justin takes a liking to Cowper, and wishes to establish him as his heir and successor, if he is willing to cooperate. But Cowper's thoughts are only of escape, and he watches for opportunities to discover the secrets of this nefarious wizard. One night, he spies Justin disappearing down a secret passageway, and following the old man, finds that the island is honeycombed with caves and man-made tunnels. Justin keeps control over the inhabitants by means of a natural gas which permeates the land; without the antidote, which the old man prepares from a hidden spring, no one on the isle could survive more than a month.

George frees one of Justin's captives, who seeks out the Lord, and hangs him from the nearest beam. Then Cowper, his friends, and his lover prepare to leave the Land of the Living Dead, having distributed to selected officials printed instructions on making the antidote. This novel is an unusual variation on the lost-race theme, in which the "race" is actually European, the island actually providing the fantastic element in the story.

"Ganpat," pseud. of Martin Gompertz. *Adventures in Sakaeland, Comprising Harilek: A Romance, and Wrexham's Romance.* New York: Arno Press, 1978.

Deep in the heart of Asia, somewhere in the middle of the great deserts north of the Himalayas, lies the walled plateau of Sakaeland, watered and green and lovely, and populated with a race partially descended from an ancient band of Greeks. Harry Lake, John Wrexham, and Alec Forsyth, ex-English soldiers back from a spell in India, follow the leads left by Wrexham's ancestor, another John Wrexham, who had traversed the deserts in 1822, and found a narrow defile leading to a gate fronted by scores of rotting bodies. But Wrexham's party had been killed either by arrows or the elements, and no one believed his story as recounted in his crumbling diary.

Now the three explorers follow these slim clues, and mount an expedition into the desert. After weeks of hardship and blowing sand, they spy a snow-capped mountain in the distance, and soon reach the high rock walls surrounding the plateau. The only entrance is guarded by a gate which spews missiles at anyone approaching; there, they rescue a princess left to die, and follow a course around the walls, until they reach a point where they can crawl up the remaining distance and return her to her home.

Sakaeland is divided into several locales controlled by different tribes. In *Harilek*, the three white men join forces with the Blue Sakae to route the Shamans who have subverted the Brown Sakae, and threaten to overrun the entire land. In *Wrexham's Romance*, John becomes enamored of a princess in Momirat, part of the Green Sakae, and defeats Zorlas, Lord of the Sera Laghara, who seeks dominion over all the tribes by playing one off against the other. Both books are filled with action, adventure, and romance. Martin Gompertz, who wrote books under the pseudonym "Ganpat," was a British career soldier in India who retired in 1939 with the rank of Brigadier General.

Gautier, Théophile, translated by Arthur D. Hall. *Spirite: A Fantasy.* New York: D. Appleton, 1877.

A young French aristocrat, Guy de Malivert, finds himself growing more and more dissatisfied with mundane and material things, and longs for ideal peace and beauty. He is supposedly engaged to the influential Madame d'Ymbercourt and is the envy of French society, but he does not love her. Gradually, he begins to feel as if some sort of influence from another world is invading his mind. He meets the Baron de Feroe, a man deeply into mysticism and Swedenborgism, who tells Guy that he is being contacted by a spirit from beyond the grave. The spirit manifests itself to him at last as the ethereally beautiful face of a young girl appearing in a mirror, and Guy falls madly and hopelessly in love with her. From then on, he is a man in a dream, sleepwalking through everyday reality, waiting only for the next manifestation of "Spirite," as he names her.

Through automatic writing Guy learns that Spirite was Lavinia d'Aufideni in life, a young girl hopelessly smitten with love for him, but whom he never noticed. Unable to stand the rejection, she joined a convent, where the rigors of religious life proved too harsh for her frail body, and where she died, still longing for Guy. Her love was so great that she was given permission to return and contact him, and if his love proves equal to the test, they will eventually be united in Heaven as one soul, as they could never be on earth.

Guy promises to do anything for her, but the strain of earthly separation is great, and he decides to commit suicide to join her. She prevents him, saying that suicide would separate them forever. So unable to bear the harshness of the city, Guy travels to Greece, where he is attacked by bandits in the hills and killed, to be joined at last with his beloved "Spirite" in Paradise.

Gillmore, Inez Haynes. *Angel Island.* New York: Henry Holt, 1914.

Five men have been shipwrecked on an uninhabited island, the only survivors of a brutal storm. The bodies of the other passengers are washed ashore around them. Collecting as many of the ship's stores as they can reach, the quintet set about making a new life for themselves. But the island is a lonely place without the touch of a woman, and there seems to be no hope of rescue: the place is far off the normal shipping lanes.

Then one night Billy suddenly awakens from a sound sleep, to find a woman's face hovering inches from his eyes. Thinking it's all a dream, he stares back for a few moments and goes back to sleep. The other men begin having similar experiences, until one memorable night, when they witness a strange sight: over the waves comes a flight of what looks like five huge birds. But as the images come closer, it becomes clear that they're actually five beautiful winged women, strange hybrids with female bodies and great gossamer wings that hurl them through the air in breathtaking aerial dances.

Having shown themselves, the women begin flirting with the lonely refugees, but refuse to come close enough to earth to get caught. This dainty game continues for several months, with the men getting ever more frustrated. Finally, they all decide that it must be ended, one way or the other, so they set a trap. In a cabin they've built, the adventurers place jewels and clothing taken from the looted trunks of drowned passengers. The wing women investigate, entering the cabin after the men have withdrawn; but the door latches automatically, trapping them.

When the men return, they clip the angels' wings, grounding them indefinitely. Each couple settles down to a reasonable facsimile of married life, à la middle Americana. But one of the girls is pregnant, and when the child is born, it has small bumps on its back where the wings will sprout. And when another winged child appears, it is clear that the race of wingmen will live to fly another day.

Grant, Robert, John Boyle O'Reilly, J. S. of Dale, and John T. Wheelright. *The King's Men: A Tale of To-Morrow.* New York: Charles Scribner's Sons, 1884.

Typical of the future "historical" romances of its time, this novel tells of political intrigue in the England and America of the 1980s. Some seventeen years before the story begins, King George V of the United Kingdom is overthrown in a revolution, and Britain becomes a republic much like the

U.S., with an elected president. The king flees to America, and there attracts a group of radical royalists who want to restore the monarch to his throne. Led by a young lord named Geoffrey Ripon, the right-wingers organize a plot against the British government, but Ripon has spurned the advances of a beautiful and unscrupulous woman, Mrs. Carey, who informs the President of England of the incipient revolt. The plot is crushed, and the leaders of the royalists are either imprisoned or executed.

King George abandons his followers and returns to America, where his feeble attempts to maintain a royal style are met with contempt and ridicule. Shortly thereafter, Geoffrey and his fellows escape from a British prison, and also come to the U.S. Ripon is reunited with his lover, Mrs. Carey; her nefarious plots are revealed, and she is forced to leave the country in disgrace. Among the book's more fascinating predictions are the overthrow of the Czarist Russian government (and the terrorization of its masses), newspapers that issue from "tickers" like stock market reports, and guns that shoot electrically charged bullets.

Grautoff, Ferdinand Heinrich, writing as Parabellum. *Banzai!* Toronto: Musson Book Co., 1908.

The "yellow peril" was a subject exploited by many popular novelists of the early twentieth century. *Banzai!*, first published in Germany in 1908, forecasts a world situation remarkably similar to that of the Second World War, and anticipates in many ways the concepts of propaganda warfare developed in more modern times.

The Japanese have infiltrated the Philippines, and have begun an underground campaign against the Americans that culminates with the destruction of an American warship. Meanwhile, organized gangs of "bandits" seize railway trains and communication lines throughout the western U.S., and before the national government can react, the states of Oregon, Washington, and California are suddenly cut off from the rest of the country. The Japanese Imperial fleet sails unopposed into San Francisco harbor, as part of a series of fictitious naval war games announced in the newspapers as under the direction of Admiral Perry.

Asian soldiers suddenly appear from their hiding places, and begin patrolling the streets of the city in strength, armed with weapons shipped to them in packing cases. American ships that have been loaded by Japanese stevedores unexpectedly begin blowing up in mid-ocean, and elsewhere on the sea strange new types of battleships are seen off the western American coast. With the help of balloons and airplanes, the other major cities in the West are soon conquered, and the Japanese offer peace. But the government vows to fight on, and the country slowly begins to organize formal and guerrilla resistance. The culminating battle is fought in the Rocky Mountains, and the invaders are soundly defeated.

Graves, C. L., and E. V. Lucas. *The War of the Wenuses.* Bristol: J. W. Arrowsmith, 1898.

"No one would have believed in the first years of the twentieth century that men and modistes on this planet were being watched by intelligences greater than woman's and yet as ambitious as her own." Thus begins this witty parody of H. G. Wells's *The War of the Worlds.* The Wenuses are rather comely young women who descend to Earth in giant crinolines in search of more copious fashions. For it seems that Wenus (*i.e.*, Venus) is rapidly becoming too hot for clothes to be worn at all, and such an alarming prospect can obviously not be long tolerated by any fashion-conscious woman.

Great crowds gather around the Wenuses' first landing site in Kensington Gardens. Suddenly the crinoline bursts open, and the Wenuses stand revealed in all their beauty. As the men stare and the women voice their disapproval, the eyes of the invaders open wide, and instantaneously every man in the area is crushed by the terrible Mash-Glance of the Wenuses. The narrator only escapes because his wife has shielded him with her bulk (women are immune). The wife takes charge of the counter-campaign, and begins organizing every woman in London to march on this threat to their freedom. They surround the headquarters of the invaders, but no one appears for hours, and the army of women find themselves growing faint for lack of refreshments (women, after all, are accustomed to regular meals). The Wenuses suddenly pour out of the building with trays of tea cups, and begin passing out the irresistible beverage to every woman in sight, and (except for the narrator's wife) the entire force succumbs to the deadly Tea-Tray of the Wenuses. A second army, headed by the narrator's mother, is decimated by the notorious Red Weed, which the Wonderful Wisitors light up in some strange and unfathomable fashion, blowing the smoke directly into the faces of the defenseless Britons. All appears lost until the Wenuses discover a soap factory, and rise from the Earth in giant soap bubbles, forever leaving the scene of their brief triumph.

Green, Fitzhugh. *ZR Wins*. New York: D. Appleton, 1924.

During the early 1920s, interest in the use of dirigibles for transport and exploration ran high, and they often figured prominently in lost-race novels of that period. *ZR Wins* is such a story, beginning with an international dirigible race over the North Pole to establish the rights to a polar trade route. Millions of dollars are potentially at stake, but Lieutenant Bliss Eppley of the United States Navy has a grander dream: he believes that there is an unknown land near the pole warmed by volcanic activity that serves as the home of a lost colony of Norsemen; and he wants to use the U.S. dirigible, the *ZR-5*, to hunt for them and to claim this territory for America! But the authorities laugh at his idea; when he uncovers a plot to sabotage the race in the interests of a group of Orientals, no one will believe him—in fact, they begin to suspect *him* of being a saboteur!

Cleverly framed by his enemy, Thorne Welchor, the real spy, Bliss attempts to prove his innocence, but without success. Finally, in an attempt to stop a sabotage attempt on the *ZR-5*, he inadvertently becomes a stowaway when the dirigible takes off. He is able to prove his loyalty to the captain and crew, but too much damage has been done and the airship is forced to drop out of the race near the North Pole. Bliss and his friend McAlford leave the stranded dirigible and set out over the ice, eventually coming upon the lost land that Bliss was so sure existed. It is peopled by descendants of the lost Vikings, who have developed an advanced civilization and possess vast oil and mineral wealth. Welchor arrives and manages to turn the peaceful Norsemen against Bliss and McAlford, but the two buddies manage to expose his treachery and reinstate themselves with the populace. Bliss is vindicated when the full story is told, *ZR* wins the polar race, and the lost land becomes a United States territory.

Greer, Tom. *A Modern Daedalus*. London: Griffith, Farran, Okeden & Welsh, 1887.

The troubles in Northern Ireland are far from recent in origin. Tom Greer manages to combine an Irish rebellion with man's development of unpowered flight. John Halloran is the son of an Irish farmer. Unlike his brothers, John has always been interested in machines and inventions, and is especially fascinated with the possibility of men flying like birds. After years of experimentation, he manages to develop a winged contraption that can be strapped on one's back. But other events are happening in the meantime: tenant farmers are being evicted by their English overlords, and John's family is caught in the midst of the unrest.

John's father begs him to give his device to the incipient rebels, but the inventor refuses to allow his machine to be used as an instrument of war, and is forced to flee to England. There he astonishes press and public alike with a demonstration of his invention, and is captured by the government, who want to use it against the Irish. A revolution has now broken out, and the Britons are suffering heavy losses. But John, who wants to give the secret of flight to the world, refuses an offer of one million pounds, and is held prisoner in the Minister's chambers. Late one night he is rescued by his brother, and they fly back to Ireland after some brief instructions by John. The inventor trains a battalion of Irish rebels to use the wings, and they bomb several English ships and garrisons, inflicting a massive defeat on the British army near Belfast. The British withdraw, and Ireland becomes an independent republic.

Gregory, Jackson, writing as Quién Sabe. *Daughter of the Sun: A Tale of Adventure.* New York: Charles Scribner's Sons, 1921.

Sometimes affecting the whimsical pseudonym "Quién Sabe" ("Who Knows?"), Jackson Gregory turned out dozens of popular adventure novels in the 1920s and '30s, most of them set in the West and Southwest. A prehistoric novel, *Ru the Conqueror*, appeared under his own name in 1933. *Daughter of the Sun*, originally serialized in a Street & Smith publication from 1920-1921 as *The Treasure of the Hills*, is an action-packed and unusual variation on the lost-race theme.

Jim "Headlong" Kendric, a handsome and reckless adventurer, gambler, and soldier of fortune wins a large sum of money from an old enemy, Ruiz Rios, a wealthy Mexican, in a dice game. Then the Mexican's dark and mysterious female companion steps forward and challenges Kendric to one throw—all or nothing. She wins, and Kendric is wiped out! Later, she sends a message to Kendric, returning his money and asking to see him.

Fascinated and annoyed, he goes to her hotel room where he is struck by her almost inhuman beauty and seductive allure. He learns that she is Zoraida Castelmar, and when he refuses to keep the money, she asks him to become her bodyguard, promising him great wealth and—other benefits. But Jim refuses her; instead, he goes on an expedition to Baja California with his friend Twisty Barlow in search of lost Aztec treasure. However, Zoraida is not to be denied: her occult powers draw Kendric to her and to her extravagant Hacienda Montezuma, and he and Twisty find themselves prisoners of the cruel and irresistible woman, who claims to be a direct descendant of Montezuma.

She shows Jim an ancient, hidden garden guarded by ancient Aztec priests, and tells him of her dream to discover the hidden treasure and use it to proclaim herself queen of a new Aztec empire in Mexico. Again, Jim refuses her offer to share her mad dream with him and barely manages to escape her wrath, taking with him a young girl, Betty Gordon, whom he has come to love. Jim and Betty are tracked and cornered in a cave in the hills by Zoraida and Rios, but their pursuers fall into an ancient trap guarding the hidden gold.

Griffith, George. *A Honeymoon in Space.* London: C. Arthur Pearson, 1901.
The Earl of Redgrave has built an extraordinary air- and spacecraft from the plans of the late Dr. Rennick. The *Astronef* has screws to propel it through the air, plus an anti-gravity device to travel between the planets. Rennick's daughter Zaidie is traveling to England to marry a rich peer when Redgrave, her old beau, kidnaps her from an ocean liner. The earl then rushes to America at the fantastic speed of 150 mph to deliver a treaty of alliance between Britain and the U.S.

After meeting with the president, Zaidic accepts Redgrave's proposal, and they use their craft to help re-elect the leader before leaving on their honeymoon, a tour of the solar system. Their first stop, the moon, is peopled with the degenerate remains of a dying civilization, which barely survives in its deepest craters. The people of Mars, on the other hand, immediately attack the *Astronef* with a fleet of airships, and the couple is forced to destroy much of the fleet before the warlike creatures withdraw. The Martians speak English, and have discarded all emotions as being inefficient.

On Venus they find gentle flying people who speak in song. Fearing they may corrupt these innocent folk, the two lovers take off for Jupiter's moons, and discover an advanced and enlightened civilization on Ganymede. These highly intelligent beings live in great domes to protect them against the cold. With the greatest scientists of that race, the craft dips into Jupiter's atmosphere, and is nearly trapped by the giant planet's gravity before it can escape. The final stop on their epic voyage is Saturn, whose soupy atmosphere is filled with huge creatures that regard the travelers as just another meal. With their fuel running short, they rush through the solar system, just skimming the outer fringes of the sun, and splash down in the ocean off the South American coast. The book's portrayal of alien civilizations is quite compelling.

Griffith, George. *The Mummy and Miss Nitocris: A Phantasy of the Fourth Dimension.* London: T. Werner Laurie, 1906.

Professor Franklin Marmion, a renowned Egyptologist, has located the mummy of Queen Nitocris, daughter of the great Pharaoh Rameses, and has had it brought to his home in London. One evening, he is startled by the appearance of the queen's spirit, which bears an uncanny resemblance to his own daughter, also named Nitocris. The phantom tells Marmion that he is the reincarnation of Ma-Rimon, priest of Amen-Ra in the ancient Egyptian city of Memphis, and that time is meaningless to the Elect. The professor uses his newly revealed knowledge to relive the past.

After the death of Rameses, Nitocris, heir to the double crown, had been forced to marry Menkau-Ra the Conqueror, although she loved another, Prince Nefer, who had been murdered by his rival. The queen exacted her revenge at the bridal feast, when she loosed the waters of the Nile, drowning herself and her enemies in one great debacle. But the spirits of the dead live on in other bodies, to play out the cycle once again. Nitocris Marmion is the re-embodied queen, and the other players include Marmion, Phadrig Amena the Adept (Anemen-Ha the High Priest of Memphis), Prince Oscar Oscarovitch (Menkau-Ra), and Mark Merrill (Nefer), Nitocris's suitor.

The Russian, who has visions of becoming the new tsar, is a thoroughly ruthless man. He uses the occult powers of Phadrig to murder his chief rival, Prince Emil Rudolf yon Zastrow; and then sets out to seduce the girl, and eliminate her father and lover. The professor is trapped aboard the prince's yacht, and is tossed overboard in chains. All appears lost until Marmion, who has escaped through the fourth dimension, confronts Phadrig directly, and the former High Priest literally melts away before the astonished eyes of the police. Oscarovitch, who has apparently forced the beautiful girl to marry him, goes to his bridal bed to discover the decaying corpse of the mummy lying on the sheets; when they finally break down the door, they find the man who would have been Emperor of all the Russias gibbering like a mad monkey, and scraping up handfuls of brown dust off the stained sheets. Merrill and the girl are reunited with Marmion, and the drama ends.

Griffith, George. *The Romance of Golden Star*. London: F. V. White, 1897.

Although virtually unknown in the United States and almost completely eclipsed in Britain by the career of his contemporary, H. G. Wells, George Griffith was at one time the leading science-fiction author in England. When Wells's *The Time Machine* appeared in 1895, Griffith lost this lead and upon publication of *The War of the Worlds* in 1898, his star was occulted for good. Wells had ambivalent feelings of respect, contempt, and envy for Griffith, saying of himself in a letter to Arnold Bennett in 1902, "...I class with George Griffith as a purveyor of wild 'pseudo' scientific extravaganza," and acknowledging a debt to Griffith's earlier future war romance, *The Outlaws of the Air* (1895) in his own *The War in the Air* (1908).

Griffith had neither Wells's literary talent nor his originality, and most of his writing was heavily derivative of successful or earlier contemporary authors such as Edwin Lester Arnold, Jules Verne, Edward Bulwer-Lytton, and H. Rider Haggard. This latter author's outstanding lost-race novel, *Heart of the World*, was serialized in *Pearson's Magazine* in 1894 and 1895, and its success, together with Griffith's recent travels in Peru, led him to produce his own version of the lost-race concept, serialized in *Short Stories* magazine in 1895 as *Golden Star*.

The 360-year-old mummy of Vilcaroya, an Inca prince, is revived by two English scientists, Dr. Laurens Djama and Prof. Martin Lamson, and leads them to the hidden underground treasure chambers of the Inca in Peru. Vilcaroya promises them a large portion of the treasure if they will also restore to life his sister-bride, Golden Star, placed in suspended animation with him. This is done, and Vilcaroya is astounded to see that she is almost the exact image of Djama's sister Ruth, whom the Inca prince now loves. Djama attempts to betray Vilcaroya and foil his plot to recapture Peru for the Inca descendants, but Djama commits suicide and Vilcaroya unites the people of South America, restoring Peru to Indian rule.

Hadley, George, as anonymous author. *Argal; or, The Silver Devil: Being the Adventures of an Evil Spirit, Comprising a Series of Interesting Anecdotes in Public and Private Life, with Which the Demon Became Acquainted in Various Parts of the World, During His Confinement in the Metalline Substance to Which He Was Condemned, Related by Himself.* London: T. Vernon, 1793, 2 vols.

Like Charles Johnstone's *Chrysal, Argal; or, The Silver Devil* is a satirical novel designed to expose the foibles of British society in the eighteenth century.

Two Jewish moneylenders, Shadrack Solomons and Abednego Manasses, buy a number of silver objects from a thief, and begin melting them down in their shop's furnace. Included with the loot is a silver crown emblazoned with the figure of a hanged man. Tossing the piece into their crucible, they are astonished when a small column of black smoke suddenly issues forth from the fire, and the crown drops unharmed onto the table. A voice shakes the room: "I am the demon Ashtaroth, condemned by the inevitable decrees of fate to suffer for the apparent neglect of which I was not guilty."

During the time of King Charles I of England, he goes on to say, he was assigned the task of persuading that prince to marry a Catholic, contrary to the laws of the land, and to this end secreted himself in a crucifix. Unfortunately, his mission failed, and the devil Moloch had him condemned to spend an interminable period confined in the cross's metal, in whatever form it might take during the ensuing years. The demon proceeds to give the two Jews his history during the next one hundred years, as he passed from person to person, and was converted into several different forms. But just as he is finishing one story, Ashtaroth suddenly receives a summons from the infernal caverns, where a vast jubilee is about to begin. He urges his saviors to maintain his habitation so he may return again in a month, and then vanishes, with a noise like the rushing of the wind, or the enormous bellows of a Cyclopean forge.

Haggard, H(enry) Rider. *Allan and the Ice Gods: A Tale of Beginnings.* London: Hutchinson, 1927.

Sir Henry Rider Haggard first introduced his famous character, Allan Quatermain, in the bestselling novel, *King Solomon's Mines* (1885), then went on to write over a dozen more works of fantasy and African adventure featuring the white hunter. In *Allan and the Ice-Gods*, written toward the end of Haggard's life and published posthumously, he sends Allan's spirit back through time, by the use of a mystic herb called "Taduki," to relive a previous incarnation as Wi the Hunter, leader of a tribe of prehistoric men during the Ice Age.

As Wi, Allan defeats Henga, tyrannical leader of the tribe, and becomes Chief. Wi gives the tribe new laws and saves them from a saber-tooth tiger, which he and his friend Pag manage to kill. Then Wi turns his attention to the gravest danger facing the tribe: the great glacier above their valley is moving faster than ever before, and now threatens to engulf their entire forest home. He must somehow devise a method of moving the entire tribe to safety.

A strange and beautiful woman—Laleela, the Sea-Witch—appears in a boat, and Wi rescues her and gives her shelter with the tribe, against the wishes of many. She is wise and has strange powers and great courage, and despite his wishes, Wi falls in love with her. Twice she saves his life, and finally, in the spring, when the tribe's wizard demands the yearly blood sacrifice to the Ice-Gods, Wi refuses, denouncing the gods as evil. Before the enraged tribe can react, most of them are destroyed by a gigantic avalanche when the tip of the glacier breaks off. Only Wi, Pag, Laleela, and a few others escape towards new lands in Laleela's boat. At this point, the drug wears off and Allan's senses return to the present.

Haggard, H. Rider. *The Mahatma and the Hare: A Dream Story.* London: Longmans, Green, 1911.

Two of the subjects that most interested Sir Henry Rider Haggard throughout his long writing career were the occult and agrarian reform. The former is reflected in many of his novels, particularly those dealing with "She," his most notable character, and with ancient Egypt; the latter he dealt with primarily in his nonfiction books. Rarely did the two interests come together, as they did in his charming dream-fantasy, *The Mahatma and the Hare*. In 1904 Haggard experienced an unusual prophetic dream which correctly foretold the death of his retriever dog; as a result, Haggard foreswore hunting and the other blood sports so dear to the Englishman and was thereafter a crusader against them.

In 1911, after reading two newspaper clippings dealing with hunters' cruelties to captured hares, Haggard had another dream which suggested the present story to him. His friend Rudyard Kipling thought it a fine idea for a book, and had a hand in plotting it, as he did several of Haggard's novels. Thomas Hardy, whose similar views on the ruin of agriculture and rural life in England were powerfully expressed in his novels, wrote Haggard about *The Mahatma*, calling it "a strangely attractive book.... I hope very many people will read the book, and be as much moved by it as I was and am."

The narrator of the story is a despondent writer on the verge of suicide who is saved by a man named Jorsen, a student of the occult, who helps the writer recover his self-respect and teaches him about reincarnation, the Law of Karma and other supernatural lore. The writer then has a dream: on the road to Heaven he meets a hare who tells him of the terror and pain he experienced at the hands of cruel hunters before finally being torn apart by dogs. The author, who pseudonymously calls himself "Mahatma," then hears the hunter's side of the story from the hare's nemesis, who dies as a result of the last pursuit of the hare. The tale is a powerful indictment of the cruelty of man to animals and may have been a seminal influence on Richard Adams's later fantasy, *Watership Down*.

Haggard, H(enry) Rider. *When the World Shook: Being an Account of the Great Adventure of Bastin, Bickley, and Arbuthnot.* London: Cassell, 1919.

This novel is interesting as Haggard's only true venture into the SF field, and it also embodies his favorite themes of immortality and reincarnation. Humphrey Arbuthnot and his two friends are marooned on a Pacific island whose inhabitants worship the terrible god Oro. Part of the land is taboo, being regarded by the natives as the holy sanctuary of their deity. The men's curiosity about this region causes trouble, and they are forced to flee to the sacred ground, where the savages will not follow. There, deep within a cave, the explorers find the remains of an advanced civilization of incredible antiquity, including the bodies of two humans preserved in crystal coffins.

When the coffins are opened, Oro and his daughter Yva are revived, having been kept in suspended animation for 250,000 years. In that ancient time, the final war had been fought by the god-men who inhabited the earth, and Lord Oro had destroyed his enemies and all of civilization by changing the balance of the world, and sinking all the inhabited continents. Oro finds the modern world as corrupt and warlike as his own, and vows to destroy civilization once again, thus giving mankind a new start. In the center of the world, the great Balance, a mountain of stone that spins eternally through the Earth's core, is approaching a point where it can be diverted onto a new path. As Oro prepares to use his device, Yva flings her body in front of the ray, and sacrifices her life so the world may be saved. The men return to England, and Oro leaves humanity to its own destiny.

Haggard, H. Rider. *Wisdom's Daughter: The Life and Love Story of She-Who-Must-Be-Obeyed.* London: Hutchinson, 1923.

With the publication of his immortal masterpiece of fantasy, *She*, in 1886, Sir Henry Rider Haggard created an entire sub-genre of science fiction, the lost-race novel, setting the pattern for hundreds of imitations and variations on this fascinating theme. Haggard's tales of adventure and romance in exotic locales and ancient ages have enthralled and influenced dozens of writers for almost a century, including such notables as Rudyard Kipling, Robert Louis Stevenson, C. S. Lewis, H. P. Lovecraft, A. Merritt, Graham Greene, and Henry Miller. This last author was so impressed by Haggard—and in particular, by *She*—that he devoted two entire chapters of his work, *The Books in My Life*, to Haggard.

Haggard himself seemed profoundly affected by the saga of Ayesha, "She-Who-Must-Be-Obeyed," for throughout his entire career he kept returning to his living goddess and adding to her story.

She itself tells only a small part of the tale; *Ayesha: The Return of She* (1905) and *She and Allan* (1921) add to the legend still further. Finally, toward the end of his life, Haggard completed the story with the superbly written and moving "autobiography" of Ayesha, *Wisdom's Daughter* (1923), long the most eagerly sought after and most difficult to obtain of all the "She" books. Ayesha describes her prenatal destiny as the high priestess of Isis and destroyer of kingdoms; her birth as the daughter of an Arab chieftain; the coming of her faithful teacher and friend, Noot, White Magician, mystic, and high priest of Isis; her betrayal and eventual vengeance upon Nectanebes, Pharaoh of Egypt; her destruction of the evil god Dagon; the Phoenician city of Sidon and its lecherous king, Tenes; and many other adventures and tribulations which eventually lead to her downfall and end her two-thousand-year exile as immortal queen of the ancient ruined kingdom of Kôr.

Haldane, Charlotte. *Mélusine; or, Devil Take Her! A Romantic Novel.* London: Arthur Barker, 1936.

Based very loosely on the story of Mélusine related by Jean d'Arras for Jean de Berry, son of King Jean II of France, this lively medieval romance has enough action and romance for a dozen novels. Raymond de Forests, nephew of Emory, Earl of Poitou, comes visiting his uncle with his father Henry, and Emory immediately takes a liking to the boy, so much so that he petitions his relatively impoverished brother-in-law to let him take the lad and raise him as his own son. Henry, who has two elder sons to inherit his estates, agrees, and Raymond becomes one of the family. Behind the scenes lurks the sinister figure of Owain, counselor and magician to Earl Emory.

Owain is the leader of the forces of the earth, who are fighting the Christians for domination of Europe. He arranges for Raymond to kill his foster-father accidentally on his twenty-first birthday; the boy rides away from the scene in a bereaved frenzy, eventually coming to a grotto where Mélusine, a beautiful young princess from Britain, has been placed to seduce him. Bertrand, Emory's son, succeeds to his estate, and Raymond is granted a small area which is re-named Lusignan. There Raymond and Mélusine build a large castle, the beginnings of a great state; their sons are placed in the Kingdoms of Armenia and Jerusalem, and Raymond inherits Bertrand's lands when he dies a slow death from poisoning.

Each Saturday night Mélusine must appear before the common folk in a garment made of vipers' skins to perform the rituals so necessary to her faith. The Lusignans prosper, and a younger son, Geffray, who is actually the son of Owain, is groomed to take his father's place. When Geffray kills another brother who has asked to become a monk, Raymond denounces his wife as a witch, and Mélusine throws herself through the castle window. Raymond, now broken in spirit, resigns his titles to his son and retires to the mountain fastness of Montserrat to spend the rest of his days in meditation.

Harris-Burland, J. B., writing as Harris Burland. *The Princess Thora*. Boston: Little, Brown, 1904.

Harris Burland's novel is one of the best lost-race Po-lar books ever written.

Edward Silex, a bachelor book collector, is led to Si-lent Square in London, where John Silver offers him a rare Bible in exchange for mounting an expedition to the North Pole. Silver's ward, the Princess Thora, captures Silex's at-tention, and he not only agrees to manage the expedition, but also finances it out of his personal fortune. Silver proposes an unusual assembly of twenty ships, a thousand men, nu-merous rifles, 100,000 rounds of ammunition, large guns of varying types, and a huge amount of supplies. All of this is faithfully gathered, and the vessels sail on April 27th. They assemble the expedition in a bay near Greenland and while waiting there, a huge earthquake opens a way through the ice. On the other side of the wastes lies a new continent, Astur-nia, settled by refugees from Normandy in the twelfth cen-tury.

This new land is warmed by volcanic geysers and flares, which enables it to survive the long Arctic winters. Thora's father had been murdered years before by her uncle, King Charles the Red, and Thora is the rightful heir to the throne. The first obstacle on the way to the crown is the Castle of Sancta Maria, where Count Guy de Marmorel holds sway. After a long siege, a stalemate sets in and Guy finally agrees to hand over the castle in exchange for the marriage vow of Thora; he's willing to turn traitor for a chance at the throne. The two armies combine and march on the capital, Avranches.

But the castle is well-fortified, and Silex proposes a unique solution to the problem: the river running through the valley is then dammed, and the water begins flooding the city. In a final climactic battle, the king and his sons are overwhelmed and Guy is killed. Thora is proclaimed Queen, then abdicates her throne to join her new husband John Silex in a small house on the coast.

Hartmann, Franz. *Among the Gnomes: An Occult Tale of Adventure in the Untersberg*. London: T. Fisher Unwin, 1895.

The Untersberg, in the Austrian Alps, "is known to be inhabited by certain kinds of elemental spirits of Nature, some of which are good and beneficial, others of a wicked and malicious nature, inimical to mankind." Herr Schneider joins an expedition to investigate these rumors and descends into a cave beneath the mountain. In losing his way, he finally comes upon a cavern where a mysterious light is shining. Suddenly the shape of a woman forms before his eyes: it is the Princess Adalga, daughter of the King of the Gnomes. The denizens of the inner world regard Schneider as a ghost or spirit from the real world; and to the human, the inhabitants below all shine with their own internal light.

But all is not well in the Untersberg: Schneider inadvertently allows the forces of corruption to penetrate the spirit world, and the gnomes begin driving a tunnel into the sky. The spirits of the air, entities of music and sound, fight back, causing horrendous destruction with their fluid lightning. But the gnomes, despite their dreadful losses, persist in their attack, and are driven back into their own kingdom. The symbol of evil, a great statue of a frog, is destroyed, and Schneider is restored to his own world again, wondering whether it was all just a bad dream.

This satirical tale is very critical of the pretensions of its era. Franz Hartmann is best known for his serious works on the occult, including his classic book, *Magic White and Black*.

Harvey, William Fryer. *Midnight House and Other Tales*. London: J. M. Dent & Sons, 1910.

British doctor William Fryer Harvey has often been compared to Walter de la Mare, since each frequently used the psychological ghost story as the basis of his fiction. This collection is considered by most experts to be Harvey's finest.

In "Midnight House," a spirit of evil roams abroad in the night. You should never walk "Across the Moors" alone after dark, unless you're looking for a ghost. Tradescant discovers the last remnant of a living fossil in New Zealand, and then takes his knowledge to the grave. A headstone cutter carves a name and date on a sample piece of rock, and finds them coming true during "August Heat." Little Janey owned many different dollies, but "Sambo" was different from all the rest.

In "Sarah Bennet's Possession," an ancient love affair is relived for the audience of the living. "The Tortoise" wanders about the house with a strange glitter in its eyes, almost like the look the old master gave the butler while the servant was murdering him. "The Educationalist" is an old man who finds he can predict the future lives of certain young people, but can do nothing to change what he sees.

Also included are: "The Star," "Deaf and Dumb," "Unwinding," "A Middle-Class Tragedy," "The Fern," "The Angel of Stone," "After the Flower Show," and "The Desecrator."

Hearn, Lafcadio, edited by Charles Woodward Hutson. *Fantastics and Other Fancies*. Boston: Houghton Mifflin Co., 1914.

Although these stories and sketches were not compiled until after Hearn's death in 1904, they actually were penned at the beginning of his career, during several stints as a newspaper writer for two small New Orleans newspapers, the *City Item* and the *Times-Democrat*. The tales appeared over a five-year period beginning in 1879, and at times ran weekly or monthly in the papers' columns, depending on their need for material and Hearn's free time. Charles Woodward Hutson, who edited this volume, says in his introduction:

> But it is not alone the charm that clings about all that is weird and fanciful that gives value to this early work of Hearn's. It sheds rich light upon one phase of his development, and forms an essential part of his biography; and it helps to furnish proof, along with much else of varying form and excellence, that he put forth a vast deal of literary effort in the years of his stay in New Orleans.... From a hint given him by a travelers tale, by a trivial street incident, by a couplet of verse, or a carven cameo in an antique shop, by an old legend, or a few grains of sand, his genius was able to create a series of vivid and mystical visions, more real to him and to his readers than the political contests or the personal gossip which filled the surrounding columns of print.

Hecht, Ben. *Fantazius Mallare: A Mysterious Oath.* Chicago: Covici-McGee, 1922. *The Kingdom of Evil: A Continuation of the Journal of Fantazius Mallare.* Chicago: Pascal Covici, 1924.

Fantazius Mallare first appeared in a "limited edition for private circulation only, consisting of two thousand and twenty-five numbered copies." When we consider the standards of "decency" prevalent in the literature of the 1920s, especially in this country, it is easy to see how this bizarre and outrageous work was considered by some at the time to have been the vilest pornography. Hecht's long dedication, "to my enemies," didn't help matters, and for years the book remained a much-sought-after erotic classic, not only for the dark, grotesque tale it tells, but for the incredible, tortured illustrations provided for it by author-illustrator Wallace Smith, reproduced in the present edition.

Hecht takes us into the deepest, wildest recesses of Mallare's mind—the mind of a madman, whose journal carefully recounts, step by step, his progressive descent into delusion and insanity. This book, and its even more horrifying sequel, *The Kingdom of Evil* (also published for subscription only in a limited edition of 2000 copies in 1924), are a brilliant exercise in the portrayal of the morbid, diseased world created by a madman inside his own brain, peopled with characters who are really different aspects of his own degenerating schizophrenic personality.

The influence of J.-K. Huysmans, whom Hecht much admired, is very evident in these two works, particularly Huysmans's novels, *Down There* and *Against the Grain*; and the only novel that comes close in imagination to the loathsome world of *The Kingdom of Evil* is Octave Mirbeau's *Torture Garden*. These incredible *tours-de-force* have not lost their powers to shock, and stand almost without equal in the literature of the weird and the bizarre.

Hernaman-Johnson, F. *The Polyphemes: A Story of Strange Adventures Among Strange Beings.* London: Ward, Lock, 1906.

The Polyphemes are giant ants who invade Europe with thousands of bombing airships. John Le Galliene, a doctor in His Majesty's Navy, tells the story. On duty off the South American coast, a flotilla of three ships is suddenly attacked from above, and two of the craft are destroyed before the creatures are beaten back. As they sail into their English port, Le Galliene finds England paralyzed from a series of mysterious kidnappings. By abducting officials and destroying roads, the elusive insects drive the country people back towards the large cities and population centers.

Once concentrated, the Britons are decimated when the ants poison their water supply with a clear, tasteless agent that causes the body to swell and bloat in horrible agony. A hundred million men die within the day. The navy mounts a counterattack from their last remaining base, sending out a new fleet of sixteen airships to do as much damage as possible. After a valiant struggle, the fleet is gradually overpowered by the insect craft, and Le Galliene awakens to find himself a prisoner at the ants' home base, two islands in the Pacific.

The creatures are ruled by a priesthood that sacrifices its victims to the Moon, but secretly preserves the supposed dead for a much more gruesome fate. The High Priests have discovered the secret of eternal life, which rests upon the slow extraction of the life force from intelligent beings. Trapped in a special chamber, Le Galliene finds himself aging years in a week's time and rapidly growing old as the diabolical machine does its work. Then, as the masses of ants revolt against their oppressive rulers, the doctor escapes, and the British fleet arrives just in time for the rescue. The last remnants of the priestly class destroy their own citadels rather than hand them over to the worker ants.

Heron-Allen, Edward, writing as Christopher Blayre. *The Strange Papers of Dr Blayre.* London: Philip Allan, 1932.

Edward Heron-Allen was a leading intellectual in Great Britain during the early part of this century. About 1920 he began writing a pseudonymous series of supernatural stories emanating from the mythical University of Cosmopoli, supposedly presented by a former Registrar of the school, Christopher Blayre. The first of these unusual pieces appeared in the *Anglo-French Review* under the byline "Flavius," and they were later collected in a book called *The Purple Sapphire and Other Posthumous Papers* (Philip Allan, 1921). Eleven years later the present edition was published, with four additional stories added to the earlier tales.

"The Purple Sapphire" tells the story of a cursed jewel that brings bad luck to anyone who possesses it. In "A House on the Way to Hell," the late University Librarian goes to his just reward, and finds himself in charge of a special library collecting unfinished literary classics now completed after death by the spirits of their authors. Professor Markwand invents a means of communicating with the projected spirit-image of a Venusian, "Laalila," with tragic results. "The Mirror That Remembered" brings rewards its inventor never expected. In "Purpura Lapillus," The Regius Professor of History experiences a strange vision of Roman times; Ippolito is strangled by the withered hand, the "Mano Pantea," he carries in a pouch dangling from his neck.

"The Thing That Smelt" reveals its presence to its intended victims through an overpowering odor of corruption and decay. The bite of "The Blue Cockroach" transforms an old bachelor's life for a few bright hours. "The Man Who Killed the Jew" is the story of Khartophilus, the Wandering Jew, who finally reaches an end to his travels in a little resort town on the English coast. A dying woman is possessed by "The Demon," which reanimates her body, and gives her new life. "The Book" is the key to a mysterious haunting in the library of an old mansion. Scientists examining the ruins of Markwand's destroyed laboratory find evidence of mysterious "Cosmic Dust" among the remains.

Hodder, William Reginald. *The Daughter of the Dawn: A Realistic Story of Maori Magic*. London: Jarrold & Sons, 1902.

In darkest New Zealand, the Maoris have a legend that Hinauri, last of the ancient race of Tohungas who carved out the interior of the sacred mountain, will return to overthrow the forces of evil. Years before, one of the Maori chiefs, Te Makawawa, had stolen a white woman and her unborn daughter, believing that they were marked out by the gods for a singular destiny; and now Dick Warnock, having been sent out from London to find the woman (who has inherited a fortune), comes to New Zealand to follow the traces of a path twenty years old.

The Maori tells him that the daughter, was taken at birth and later returned to her father; and that he will tell Warnock where the mother is located if they will restore the daughter to her parent. With the help of Kahikatea, an Englishman living under an assumed name, Wanaki, as he is called by the Maoris, locates the girl and her father and leads them on a journey into the interior towards the great sacred mountain. The priest of the mountain tells them Crystal, the daughter, is the reincarnated form of Hinauri. As the forces of the vile Tohungas gather to combat the return of the Hinauri, the priest, Ngaraki, uses his magic to cast down the statues of the evil ones, deep within the bowels of the mountain. Her mission accomplished, Crystal Hinauri returns to the heavens and the wizards are sent to the hells they deserve. A saddened Wanaki, who had loved the girl, returns to civilization to write his account before he too passes into the great beyond. Hodder's story is unusual in that it employs New Zealand magic and legends, a rich source rarely used in fantastic literature before or since.

Holmes, Oliver Wendell, Sr. *Elsie Venner: A Romance of Destiny.* Boston: Ticknor & Fields, 1861, 2 vols.

"Much of the best in American horror-literature has come from pens not mainly devoted to that medium," writes H. P. Lovecraft in his *Supernatural Horror in Literature.* The truth of this can readily be ascertained by a look at the works of such authors as Henry James, Ben Hecht, W. W. Jacobs, Albert Bigelow Paine, Louis Bromfield, F. Marion Crawford, and many others. An outstanding example can be found in the novel *Elsie Venner*, published in 1861 by Oliver Wendell Holmes, one of America's most distinguished men of letters and father of the great Supreme Court Justice, Oliver Wendell Holmes, Jr., who became known as "the great dissenter." Physician, teacher, scientist, poet, essayist, novelist, biographer, critic, and lecturer, the elder Holmes effected a pioneering interest in psychiatry, which he expressed in a series of three novels he called his "medicated novels."

Elsie Venner was the first of these, and has been called "a brilliant study of a schizophrenic girl," published when Sigmund Freud was only five years old! But there is more to *Venner* than psychiatry—in it Holmes tests the doctrine of "original sin" and human responsibility, and explores the dark areas of hypnotic influence, clairvoyance, and prenatal trauma as well.

Elsie Venner is a strikingly beautiful young girl of seventeen, but her beauty is wild, dark, and cold. Her eyes "glitter like diamonds," she has few friends, and many are afraid of her. She constantly wears around her neck a golden collar which is said to conceal a frightful birthmark. She speaks little, and has no one in whom to confide except her old African nurse, Sophy, who knows Elsie's fearful secret: that her mother died of snakebite incurred right before the child was born! Even Elsie's love for a handsome young schoolteacher cannot save her from her ultimate tragic destiny.

Housman, Clemence. *The Were-Wolf.* London: John Lane, The Bodley Head, 1896.

Second only to the vampire in popularity among lovers of the supernatural is the werewolf, that hapless being who changes from man (or woman) to beast when the moon is full. The subject has attracted many of the finest writers of the weird, including Algernon Blackwood, Ambrose Bierce, Frederick Marryat, Eugene Field, Erckmann-Chatrian (see *The Man-Wolf and Other Tales*), Alexandre Dumas, and many others. But surely no one has treated lycanthropy with more beauty or literacy than Clemence Housman in her small classic, *The Were-Wolf*. H. P. Lovecraft, in his *Supernatural Horror in Literature*, said that this tale "attains a high degree of gruesome tension and achieves to some extent the atmosphere of authentic folklore." Montague Summers, in his book *The Werewolf*, discusses the story in more detail:

> Clemence Housman's exquisite prose poem, *The Were-Wolf*, 1896, reprinted from *Atalanta*, is told with feeling that is as rare as it is beautiful. Without a harrowing detail we are brought fully to realize the terror of "the dreadful Thing in their midst," White Fell, the foul wolfden in woman's shape. Very poignant is the end of Christian, who out of his great love for Sweyn lays down his life amid the pathless ice and snows in order that his brother might be saved from the caress of

the werewolf. By Christian's death the Thing dies. "The great grim jaws had a savage grin, though dead-stiff." And Sweyn's reason totters upon its seat when he thinks of the kiss he had so fondly printed there.

This strange tale of horror was illustrated by the author's husband, the well-known children's writer, Laurence Housman.

Hyne, C. J. Cutcliffe. *Empire of the World*. London: Everett & Co., 1910.

Cutcliffe Hyne, author of *The Lost Continent*, here narrates the story of a lone scientist pacifying the world with a fabulous new power. John Bryn-Scarlett, M.P., has developed a disintegrating ray that destroys iron. A torpedo boat being delivered to Germany suddenly sinks beneath the Thames, and in Germany itself the great battleship *Kaiser Charlemayne* just as quickly loses its bottom on a mud bank in the Kiel Canal. Bryn-Scarlett warns the world that unless the rest of the German fleet stays in the Canal, he will destroy every ship that tries to leave. But Bryn-Scarlett has been temporarily evicted by his landlady for not paying the rent, and the Germans head for the open sea.

Soon, however, the world hears again from the scientist, for he has found a way to tap into the main telephone terminals. He tells the media that disobedience of his commands will result in dire consequences. A London newspaper which calls his bluff finds its presses melted into sludge the next morning. An American senator speaks out against the "Imperator Mundi," and finds his trans-Atlantic cable company suddenly without a cable. All opposition is crushed. Countries refusing to submit discover their rail lines and telegraph wires dissolving into dust. The German Confederation is forced to disband, and all the nations of the world pledge allegiance to their new master. And John Bryn-Scarlett, still poor and unknown, marries his girl and settles down to a long, anonymous reign as the Emperor of the World.

In the Future: A Sketch in Ten Chapters, anonymously published. Hampstead, England: "Express" Office, 1875. *In the Future* is typical of the SF writing of the late 1900s. The novel is based largely on religious doctrines, but with a science-fiction twist. The book is set in futuristic London, with clinical cities of cleanliness and uniformity— cities that are crime-free, pollution-free, and traffic-free. The European Revolution has leveled Rome. Hatred of classes, strife between capital and laborer, bitterness of race against race, and antagonism of creeds have culminated and destroyed the social and political systems of the "Old World." The Ten-Fold King, who is supreme ruler of the Babel-Rome Empire, is in command. He has brought tranquility, order, a loftier civilization, and a religion that is centered on himself.

In this new society, social development is such that no man may wage war with other men on his own account— even in a just cause. No man is permitted to profess a singular or abnormal system of religion. The Divine rule of The King and his sacred order of the realm cannot be broken; thus, his reign is a truly despotic one. Society is ruled by a strict caste system and "The State" is the only great capitalist. In this future world, freedom is synonymous with sedition. To counterbalance this tyranny is Meredith the Christian, whose kindness, wisdom, and devotion to his religion spurs his co-religionists to fight for their individualism and freedom to be Christians.

Ingram, Eleanor M. *The Thing from the Lake*. Philadelphia: J. B. Lippincott, 1921.

Roger Locke, a well-known writer of popular songs, buys the old Michell property in rural Connecticut, determined to find a secluded refuge from the pressures of New York. During his first night in the house, he wakes to find a braid of hair trailing through his open hand. A woman's soft voice warns him to leave the house while he can; but when he manages to find the light, the girl has vanished, leaving the cut length of hair dangling by his bed. Later that night Locke hears a strange sucking sound emanating from the lake behind the house. He smells a hideous stench pouring in through the window. Then he realizes that Something is watching him with the covetousness of a beast for its prey. Roger manages to throw off the beast's hypnotic pull, but realizes the creature will return again. He gradually falls in love with the girl, who returns on many occasions, but Locke is never permitted to see or touch the woman, and wonders if she exists in the flesh. The Thing also comes back, incessantly trying to force its way past the barrier of Roger's will. Locke finds a book detailing the career of a seventeenth-century witch, Desire Michell, who had been jilted by her lover, and then had destroyed him through occult powers. She called up a monster from the beyond, but had herself been overcome by its menace; the creature had then been free to prey upon succeeding family members.

Roger finds it increasingly difficult to battle the Thing, and finally manages to force the girl into the open. Desire Michell IV, last of the family, lives in a convent nearby. Locke's love for the woman makes it imperative that he find a way to break the cycle, and they face the menace together as waves of icy cold foulness break over the two frail humans. Locke offers his life to the creature in exchange for the girl's, and the debt is finally paid. The Thing is thrust back into its nether world, the breach repaired, and the two lovers are saved forever.

Here is a story which may well have influenced (or at least anticipated) the writing of H. P. Lovecraft.

James, M(ontague) R(hodes). *The Five Jars.* London: Edward Arnold, 1922.

Peter Penzoldt, in his book *The Supernatural in Fiction*, called Montague Rhodes James "the most successful ghost-story writer of this century." H. P. Lovecraft said of him: "He is gifted with an almost diabolic power of calling horror by gentle steps from the midst of prosaic daily life." Most of James's work consisted of short stories, but he did write one little-known novel, *The Five Jars,* which was published originally for the younger crowd, but can be enjoyed by readers of all ages.

The narrator follows the instructions of a murmuring brook, and finds a box containing five magic jars. He leaves the container on a table near the window, and the moonlight shining on the metal opens it with a snap. The glass containers are marked with Latin words indicating the eyes, ears, tongue, forehead, and chest, but the narrator, uncertain how to use them, goes off to bed. In a dream he sees an ancient Roman applying the creams, and, following his instructions, touches the contents of the first jar to his ears. Immediately, he finds himself understanding the languages of the animals. On each successive night he opens another jar, and his powers increase correspondingly: "The Eyes" allows him to see the little people and their dwellings, and warns him of the "Others," who seek the jars for their own nefarious schemes; "The Tongue" gives him the power to talk with the animals, spirits, and little creatures he has already seen; "The Forehead" allows him to envision past events as they had occurred at a particular location; "The Chest" gives him the power to reduce his size at will, and visit his little friends in their own homes. But each night the attacks of "The Others" grow stronger, and on the final night, swarms of bats gather round his house. Using hoses and horseshoes, the author dampens the magic of his enemies, vanquishes them completely, and is confirmed as the master of the Five Jars.

Jane, Fred T. *The Violet Flame: A Story of Armageddon and After.* London: Ward, Lock, 1899.

The violet flame is an invention of Professor Mirzarbeau, a mad scientist in the grand tradition. The "flame" disintegrates everything it touches, and Mirzarbeau uses his weapon to make himself dictator of England. The Professor draws his power from an apparatus that can pick up the thoughts of the Earth, which he regards as a living organism. Those who support his rule are provided with green disks to protect them from the effects of the ray. Once placed on the forehead, hand, or other parts of the body, the disks are nearly impossible to remove by the uninitiated. Mirzarbeau has also altered the path of a giant comet, which he threatens to unleash upon the world unless mankind submits to his rule.

Lester, who has closely followed the Frenchman's career, believes the scientist can be destroyed if someone can manage to gain access to his laboratory, which is protected by the flame. The government agrees to try his scheme, which involves digging a tunnel underground from the nearest sewer line. But as the workmen near the area of the house, they come up against a grey stone wall of impenetrable material. Suddenly, part of the wall slides to one side, and Mirzarbeau himself welcomes the invaders. One of the soldiers fires at the scientist, slightly wounding him before the door shuts. Shortly thereafter the Professor is killed by one of his own colleagues, and the great comet is headed directly for the Earth. As the comet grows brighter, tides rise to immense heights, covering all but the tallest buildings, and then recede, leaving millions dead. The air is filled with purple lightning, and everywhere men riot and kill.

Lester and his lover take refuge in a skyscraper, and are then caught up in a savage crowd. Suddenly everyone vanishes except the man and woman, both of whom are wearing the protective disks. The world has become an endless plain of grey miniatures. Only one building still survives, the laboratory which was marked with the green circles. With the resources they find in the lab, the last two people on Earth set about restoring civilization.

Jefferies, Richard. *After London; or, Wild England.* London: Cassell, 1885.

The only science-fiction novel by a noted British naturalist, this book was also one of the earliest to project a world of the distant future reduced to barbarism by some unknown cataclysm. Part 1, "The Relapse into Barbarism," describes this future world in great detail, as the writer tries to piece together the story of how civilization returned to the primitive. All records have been destroyed, and all knowledge of the arts and sciences is lost. Some lands no longer survive and there are legends of geologic convulsions, perhaps caused by a comet passing close to Earth. A vast, polluted lake exists in the center of England over the site of the ancient city of London. The few men left alive are just emerging from complete savagery into a semi-feudal social system.

In the second part, "Wild England," Sir Felix, eldest son of the Baron of Aquila, undertakes a long, hazardous journey across England to the stagnant marshes and fetid waters covering the ruins of London. He finds human skeletons and crumbling, phosphorescent walls, and is nearly overcome by the lethal miasma from the polluted waters. Fortunately, he is able to find his way out of the swamp, and when his strength returns, Felix helps a tribe of shepherds fight off a wandering band of gypsies. In gratitude, the shepherds elect him their chief, and Felix decides to stay and build a fortress city for himself and Aurora, who waits for him to return from his quest. *After London* is remarkable for its vivid and prophetic portrayal of how the ravages of pollution can affect the beauty of nature.

Johnstone, Charles, writing as "An Adept." *Chrysal; or, The Adventures of a Guinea: Wherein Are Exhibited Views of Several Striking Scenes, with Curious and Interested Anecdotes of the Most Noted Persons in Every Rank of Life, Whose Hands It Passed Through, in America, England, Holland, Germany, and Portugal.* London: T. Becket, 1760, 2 vols.

The occult experimenter has fasted for many a day, purifying his body from every excess and encumbrance; and his efforts are finally rewarded: the spirit of a heavenly being comes forth from the shining gold coin! A great yellow glow fills the room, and an ethereal voice announces the arrival of Chrysal, a member of the superior order of beings animating the monarch of metals. Among the spirit's many powers is the remarkable ability to enter the hearts and minds of each possessor of the coin, revealing the secrets and personal histories of any who touch it. What's more, Chrysal can make any human desire the gold to such a degree that mortal flesh will do anything to possess it, thereby facilitating the being's travels from person to person. This is why men seem to love an inanimate object so much; the spirit of the gold has fastened itself on the man, and not vice versa, and the larger the mass of metal, the more powerful the spirit.

Chrysal relates how he/she (spirits are both male and female) was dug up in Peru, and was then passed by the miner to a priest in confession. After relating both men's histories, the spirit tells how it embarked for Europe on an English man-of-war, and, having arrived in London, passed from hand to hand, touching both the mighty and the lowly. The adept is simultaneously given the histories of a noble British lord and a celebrated lady, and is also entertained with a running account of English politics and societal foibles. No one escapes Chrysal's critical eye. Finally, the spirit passes from a pawnbroker to the narrator, and is so pleased at being able to relate its story, that in return it decides to give the adept the secret of occult knowledge. But the experimenter, being only human, has gaseous indigestion, and can hold back the noxious fumes no longer. The spirit of Chrysal, mortally offended by this horrendous breach of ethics, vanishes into thin air.

Keller, David H. *The Devil and the Doctor.* New York: Simon & Schuster, 1940.

American doctor David H. Keller wrote a great many supernatural stories for *Weird Tales* during the 1920s and 1930s, but this is one of his few forays into humorous fantasy. Jacob Hubler, a retired M.D., runs a small bookstore in Stroudsburg. One day, a stranger walks through his doors, and expresses interest in Hubler's collection of books on the devil. When the doctor mentions that he someday hopes to write the demon's biography, the stranger offers his assistance, and begins retelling the story of creation, with a few new twists.

"God" and the "Devil" are really twin brothers, he says, and they've been rivals ever since their father left them a little creative material to play with. His elder brother then had the audacity to make a creature in his own image. The poor thing was so lonely that the devil used his portion to make a mate for it. When brother complained, he was given the privilege of being called "god" by the creatures, and the younger son was left in the role of pariah, cursed by humans down through the ages whenever he tried to enlighten them with his knowledge.

Robin Goodfellow, as the stranger calls himself, manages to pull a few strings behind the scenes to enable Jacob to achieve his one ambition in life, retirement on a farm. He also provides the unsuspecting doctor with a young, pretty wife who loves him, and a chest of gold Hubler manages to stumble across quite by accident. Goodfellow is a fine companion, but he does have a few oddities about him: he loves fires, never seems to cast a shadow, dispenses radium-impregnated double eagles seemingly at will, and has a habit of disappearing rather abruptly when certain things are said in his presence. But not everyone likes the devil, and the president of the local church mounts a campaign to run them both out of the valley. But at the moment of confrontation, Goodfellow is surrounded by white-cloaked physicians who claim he's an escaped lunatic from a hospital in upstate New York. Of course, when Jacob checks with the medical authorities there, he's told that the hospital never existed.

Kerby, Susan Alice. *Miss Carter and the Ifrit*. London: Hutchinson, 1945.

Georgina Carter, an old maid of forty-seven living in the London of World War II, is unhappy with her life, which seems to go from one rut to another. One evening, while burning a log in her fireplace, she suddenly finds a strangely-garbed foreigner standing before her. Abu Shihab, for such is his name, is an Ifrit, one of the order of demons in Muslim mythology which was banished by the great king Sulayman (Solomon) for their evil deeds. Each of the offenders has had to serve a term imprisoned in an inanimate object; Abu Shihab was walled up in a young tree on a lonely hill, until such time as he would be released by the purifying action of fire. Now he is Miss Carter's slave, to give her whatever she desires.

But Georgina's needs are simple, and she finds herself constantly forced to restrain the enthusiasm of a spirit who has literally been bottled up for over three millennia. The Ifrit transforms her plainly decorated flat into a princess's dream, and provides her with more sweetmeats and exotic drinks than she knows what to do with. He also arranges for her to meet her old beau, Richard Taylor, an American officer now posted in the British Isles. The two rekindle the affection they once held for each other, and Georgina finds herself falling in love with the handsome major. When Richard proposes, she joyously accepts, but is left with the question of what to do with the boyish affections of the Muslim spirit.

But Abu Shihab has also matured, and is ready to go on to higher things. Miss Carter recites the words: "Abu Shihab, go in peace. By the lesson you have learned in your captivity you are released now and forever from all bondage to mankind, for it was your hatred which made you a slave. And only by hatred can you be enslaved again." And the Ifrit dissolves into mist.

Kingsmill, Hugh. *The Return of William Shakespeare*. London: Duckworth, 1929.

Albert Henry Butt, a rather small, insignificant scientist, has discovered a means to reintegrate the bodies of the dead and bring them back to life. His power extends to any man or woman who has ever lived, as long as he can determine the exact date and place of the person's birth. A fragment of the original is not required. Melmoth immediately sees the possibilities in Butt's invention, and urges him to try the process on humans. And who better than the great sage himself, William Shakespeare? After all, Shakespeare's life, despite the most intense searching by scholars, remains largely shrouded in mystery; being able to talk with the man himself after 350 years in the grave would produce the greatest possible publicity in the newspapers. Further experiments on smaller animals indicate that a man can be resuscitated at any date in his life.

After carefully weighing the statements of the critics, Melmoth picks 1607, a critical date in Shakespeare's career, when he reached the peak of his powers. The process works. But Shakespeare proves unable to cope with the burdens of modern life and his own re-existence, and he suffers an emotional breakdown. The scholars, it seems, were wrong: Shakespeare had been in the midst of a creative *depression* in 1607. By the time he recovers his equanimity, the inevitable physical decay wrought by the process has begun to set in.

The Bard dies soon thereafter, never having been seen by the world he was supposed to enlighten.

Knowles, Vernon. *Sapphires: Here and Otherwise, and Silver Nutmegs*. New York: Arno Press, 1978.

Vernon Knowles wrote four collections of fantasy stories, one of which, *The Street of Queer Houses and Other Tales*, was reprinted by Arno Press in 1976. This compilation of two other collections from the 1920s preserves, together with the earlier book, the best of the author's fantastic fiction.

The stories include: "The Ladder," a classic short novel of an Oriental magic ladder and its effect on a small English town; "The Chimpanzee," which tells how the animal world tried to civilize mankind; "The Gong of Transportation," a parable of the young King Merea, and how he created his dream land; "The Great Onion," the story of a vegetable out of control; "The Door with the Three Padlocks," in which Orinda finds her love in a most unexpected place; "The Shop in the Off-Street," or how Mr. Beckett escaped his humdrum world and flew away into fantasyland; "The Birds," a cruel little tale which demonstrates why it's not nice to fool Mother Nature; "The Painter of Trees," who paints exactly what he sees; and many others, including: "The River and the Road," "The City of All Cities," "The Land of Ideas," "The Road to Tolbrisa," "The Land of No More Tears," "The Triumph of the Tree," "A Conversation," and "A Set of Chinese Boxes."

Knowles, Vernon. *The Street of Queer Houses and Other Tales*. New York: Boullion-Biggs, 1924.

Vernon Knowles writes of the strange people who exist just beyond the peripheries of everyday life. The avenue called John Street, also known as "The Street of Queer Houses," had been built by a very eccentric architect, who had designed the buildings to reflect the peculiarities of their inhabitants. And the dwellers on John Street are very odd indeed. "The Weeping God" is the strength of the southern peoples of Poscoma-Ena, until the northerners invade in jealousy. To pass through "The House of Yesterdays," one pays a price: ten years of life for each door opened onto the past. "The Three Gods" of Ragana are protection against any invader, provided they are faced in the right direction. "The Pendant" brings good fortune to its wearer, unless you try to take it off. In "A Matter of Characterization," the good author is visited one night by his own creations. "The Author Who Entered His Own Ms." finds it a sure road to death. Keninta's beautiful wife has died, but she can be brought back to life again, in a manner of speaking. "The Man Troubled by His Own Shadow" finds a way to dispense with it, to his deep regret. "The Book of a Thousand Answers" protects its guardian, even from the flames. "The Idealist" generously gives everyone on Earth their wish, and finds they all want him dead. "The Broken Statue" is the key to Paul's dreams, and so Anne stands in, permanently. "The House That Took Revenge" keeps inching towards the cliffs, until one morning it finally goes over. "Honeymoon Cottage" watches over the new couple with great delight, until the pretty girl dies...twice.

Kummer, Frederic Arnold. *Shades of Hades: Ladies in Hades: A Story of Hell's Smart Set, and Gentlemen in Hades: The Story of a Damned Débutante.* New York: Arno Press, 1978.

One of the most popular books of humorous fantasy published in the 1890s was John Kendrick Bangs's *A House-Boat on the Styx* (1895), in which he assembled a heterogeneous group of the most celebrated spirits in history and literature—from Diogenes and Hamlet through Sam Johnson, Mozart, Napoleon, and George Washington—on a houseboat in Hades. The success of this volume prompted two sequels, *The Pursuit of the House-Boat* (1897) and *The Enchanted Typewriter* (1899), and many imitations during the early 1900s. Toward the end of the 1920s, Bangs's idea was cleverly revived and "modernized" in two books by Frederic Arnold Kummer, a popular novelist, playwright, and librettist for several musical comedies.

Ladies in Hades and its sequel, *Gentlemen in Hades*, proved to be as popular during the late 1920s and early '30s as their predecessors had been around the turn of the century, and they went through numerous printings and editions. Despite the enormous success of these and other fantasy novels by Kummer and the fact that his son, Frederic Arnold Kummer, Jr., wrote science fiction for the pulp magazines during the 1930s and '40s, he is almost completely forgotten today.

Ladies in Hades deals with a group of the most famous women in Hell, who form a ladies' club and take turns telling their versions of what *really* happened in history. Eve, Lilith, Scheherazade, the Queen of Sheba, Delilah, Phryne, Sappho, Cleopatra, and other notorious vamps stir up such a fuss in Hades that an annoyed Satan is forced to disband the club. The sequel relates the story of a modern society belle who is killed in an auto accident and soon finds herself in bed with all the great men of history—Ben Franklin, Noah, Shakespeare, Adam, Hercules, Richard the Lion-Hearted, and many more. Eventually, she winds up in temporary charge of Hades itself when Satan decides he needs a vacation in Paris.

Large, E. C. *Asleep in the Afternoon: A Novel.* London: Jonathan Cape, 1938.

Ernest Large is one of those authors who can appropriately be termed a major "minor" writer. The author of three novels of fantastic literature, he has never had a large following; but there has always been a small group of sophisticated writers, critics, and devotees who have followed his work avidly and who regard Large as one of the principal satirical writers of his day.

His first novel, *Sugar in the Air*, featured one Charles Pry, a rather humdrum, unpretentious chemist who chanced upon one or two fortunate inventions and who is now, in this sequel, unemployed but with enough money to last him two years. He decides to use his time in writing a fantastic novel about Hugo Bloom, who has invented (in his story) a remarkable device that gives its wearer the gentle gift of sleep, accompanied by pleasant (and sometimes erotic) visions. The story of Hugo's gift to mankind, how his fictional wife Agatha uses it to create a power base for herself, and the interwoven story of Charles Pry, his wife Mary, and the way they cope with the bizarre rituals of success in the publishing world is a remarkable satirical achievement, and a wittily unique fantasy that only Large could have written.

Laurie, André. *The Conquest of the Moon: A Story of the Bayouda.* London: Sampson Low, Marston, Searle & Rivington, 1889.

Laurie's novel is a unique twist on an old theme; instead of voyaging to the Moon, as so many other adventurers have done, the heroes of this book bring the Moon to Earth. Norbert Mauny, a young French astronomer, believes he has solved the problem of exploiting the Moon. The most feasible method, he says, is to build a giant magnet, and draw the satellite near enough to our world that the distance between them is negligible. Having convinced a corporation to fund his expedition, Mauny sets off for the Sudan, where he intends to convert a large mountain of iron pyrites into the magnet he needs.

But the Sudan of the 1880s is not a very healthy place for foreigners. There are rumors of uprising and revolt, and it is said that a new religious leader, the Mahdi, will soon lead the Arab tribes against the hated infidels. As Mauny's preparations near completion, the Mahdists suddenly surround the mountain, as they have already encircled Khartoum and the famous Gordon Pasha. All appears lost until the Moon, attracted by the magnetic force, begins growing larger in the sky. After six days, the Moon fills the horizon, and the superstitious Arabs are terrified. One of the Europeans accidentally hits the wrong control lever, and the satellite jars the Earth before rebounding back into its orbit.

The adventurers awaken to find their mountain retreat now firmly lodged on the Moon's surface, with the Earth no more than a ball in the sky. Repairing the magnet and recharging their batteries will take more time than remains in the dwindling lunar day, and they are forced to stretch their supplies through the long, two-week night. As night falls, the temperature inside the laboratory begins to decrease, and continues to decline with each passing day. No fuel can be burned because of the limited oxygen supply. Finally, the sun rises again, their power is restored, and within six days the Moon has once again reached the Earth. The explorers separate from the lunar globe in a giant parachute, and find themselves back in the Sudan, where they are picked up by a British gunboat.

The most interesting part of this novel is the detailed description of the lunar surface, which is remarkably close to reality. The heroes explore the terrain in makeshift space-suits.

Le Queux, William. *The Eye of Istar: A Romance of the Land of No Return*. London: F. V. White, 1897.

With the development of military inventions that followed in the wake of the Industrial Revolution came also the erection of organized spy networks whose purpose was the theft or copying of the secret plans and documents for such inventions. The highly developed industrial nations were naturally those with the most secrets to uncover, and because of this, a new kind of thriller originated in Europe—and particularly in Britain—the spy story.

One of the first writers to exploit this new genre was William Le Queux, a journalist who had been a British Secret Service Agent before and during World War I. Calling upon his experiences, he wrote what may be the first spy novel, *Guilty Bonds*, in 1890, which has been said to have "mapped the guidelines for all subsequent British spy fiction." But Le Queux was not content to stay in one small area of writing: noting the tremendous popularity of the future-war novel, originating with the anonymous publication in 1871 of *The Battle of Dorking*, he realized that it was only a small step from the spy story to the tale of tomorrow's war. Accordingly, he produced a number of such works of his own, including one of the most controversial and best-selling of all future war novels, *The Invasion of 1910* (1906).

An incredibly prolific writer, Le Queux soon looked around for other areas of popular literature to develop, and soon discovered the lost-race novel, pioneered by Haggard's *She* in 1886. Such romances as *The Great White Queen* (1896) and *The Eye of Istar* were the result. In the latter novel, a young Arab, Zafar-Ben-A'Ziz, is saved from death and falls in love with Azala, daughter of the powerful Sultan of Sokoto. He discovers the same mysterious brand of two intertwined asps on her breast as has been emblazoned on his own chest since childhood. To solve this strange mystery, Azala sends Zafar on a mission to a lost civilization in Central Africa, where he finds the ancient and immense Babylonian city of Ea, ruled by a cruel and beautiful queen who is the direct descendant of Semiramis. She tries to enslave him, but he escapes and leads the Sultan's army back to conquer the city.

Le Queux, William. *The Great White Queen: A Tale of Treasure and Treason*. London: F. V. White, 1896.

One of the most popular forms of fantastic literature in the late nineteenth and early twentieth centuries was the lost-race novel. Inspired by the enormous success of H. Rider Haggard's African adventures (*She, King Solomon's Mines, Allan Quatermain*, etc.), dozens of writers followed his example by exploiting hitherto unexplored corners of the world. One of the best of these derivations was *The Great White Queen*.

A young English orphan, Richard Scarsmere, befriends a mysterious light-skinned African boy, Omar Sanom, while attending prep school, and learns that his friend is heir to an unknown African kingdom called Mo, the City in the Clouds. Scarsmere agrees to accompany Omar back to his kingdom, ruled by The Great White Queen, his mother. But they are betrayed by their guide, Kouaga, Grand Vizier of Mo, and fall into the hands of the queen's old enemy, the Arab slave trader Samory. The slave dealer tortures Omar to secure the secret of the fabulous treasure of Mo, but Omar remains silent.

Disgusted by the lack of cooperation, Samory sells the lads to another enemy of Mo, the black chieftain Prempeh. The boys barely escape with their lives, but finally manage to reach friendly natives willing to escort them on their long and hazardous journey to the hidden kingdom. At Mo they find the old queen hostile and crazy, changed into a cruel, bloodthirsty tyrant who now offers human sacrifices to the hideous crocodile god, Zomara. With the aid of wise old Goliba, one of the royal counselors, Omar and Scarsmere organize a revolution against the queen, and, after a terrible battle, overthrow her. Omar ascends the throne of Mo, and the crazed queen commits suicide.

Le Sage, Alain René. *The Devil on Two Sticks (Le Diable boiteux).* London: J. Thomas, 1841.

Alain René Le Sage was born about 1668 near the French town of Vannes. His first literary work consisted of translating certain letters of Calisthenes from Greek into modern French, but he remained in obscurity until he turned his pen to writing plays. His most famous novel, *Gil Blas de Santillane* (1715), was synthesized from the plots of his various dramas after he had turned his back on the stage. It is justly regarded as a classic of French literature. *Le Diable boiteux* was written in 1707, after Le Sage had seen a Spanish pamphlet on the same theme by Vélez de Guevara. Jules Janin summarizes the book in this way:

> The Devil is let loose on the city—a demon entirely French, with all the wit, the grace, and the vivacity of *Gil Blas.* Look, then, to yourselves, ye vicious and ridiculous—ye who have escaped sarcasm in the author's previous works; for by a touch of that all-powerful wand, not your houses alone, but your bosoms will be disclosed as through a glass. Beware! for Asmodeus, that terrible railler, will dart his remorseless eyes into sanctuaries which you believe to be impenetrable, and will recount to each of you his secret history. He will strike with that ivory crutch, and all doors, all hearts will fly open before him. None shall escape that vigilant observer, who, mounted on his staff, glides over roofs the most close and secure, and reveals to his companion the ambition, the jealousy, the disquietude, the cause of sleeplessness in all. Considered with regard to its wit, and to its all-embracing, all-deriding satire, as well as with respect to its excellent style, *The Devil on Two Sticks* is,

perhaps, the most truly French book in the
language; and is the only work which, after
Gil Blas, might have borne the name of
Molière.

Lee, Vernon. *For Maurice: Five Unlikely Stories.* London:
John Lane, The Bodley Head, 1927.
Violet Paget is perhaps the most underrated author of
twentieth-century horror literature. Despite having left a legacy of a couple dozen brilliant stories of the supernatural,
Vernon Lee (pseudonym of Violet Paget) remains virtually
unknown outside of the British Isles.
In "The Gods and Ritter Tanhüser," the ancient Greek
deities come out of retirement to aid Aphrodite in her pursuit
of the vain human poet, and medieval man soon learns to respect the powers of Athena and Apollo. "Marsyas in Flan-
ders" tells the legend of the famous Church of Dunes in
France, where a statue of Christ miraculously appeared in
1195, and wrought many wonders when the stubborn priests
tried to attach it to a cross against its will.
Don Juan Gusman del Pulgar vows to hold "The Virgin of the Seven Daggers" as the fairest of women if she will
promise him redemption; his resolution is tested when he
discovers a Moorish princess who has been entranced for 400
years. "Winthrop's Discovery" of a curious painting of a
murdered singer leads him to the scene of the crime, a decaying mansion where the spirit of the performer appears on the
anniversary of his death. When the Count's wife dies in
childbirth, the bereaved nobleman fashions a life-sized
manikin of his bride to keep him company; the Count eventually dies, but "The Doll" lives on for another hundred
years.

Leroux, Gaston. *The Bride of the Sun.* New York:
McBride, Nast, 1915.
Although he wrote over fifty books during his lifetime, French author Gaston Leroux is known in this country
today for only one—but that one is a classic of mystery and
horror almost as familiar to us as *Dracula* and *Frankenstein—The Phantom of the Opera.* First published in France

in 1910 and in this country the following year, it has been filmed many times (most notably as a Lon Chaney silent film in 1925) and often parodied (as in *The Phantom of the Paradise*). It has also appeared as a hit musical by Andrew Lloyd Webber. A well-known journalist and popular author in France in the early 1900s, Leroux went on to produce many other novels of mystery, detection (including the classic locked-room novel, *The Mystery of the Yellow Room* [1907], which John Dickson Carr considered "the best detective tale ever written"), fantasy, and science fiction. He even tried his hand at a kind of lost-race novel, serialized in a French magazine in 1912 and published in hardcover in 1913 as *L'Épouse du soleil*.

Dick Montgomery and his irascible, absent-minded archaeologist uncle, Francis Montgomery, come to Peru where Dick hopes to marry his fiancée, Maria-Teresa de la Torre, daughter of a proud Spanish marquis. Because of their insolent attitude, Maria-Teresa is forced to dismiss a group of Quichua Indians, including Huascar, who has always been a faithful friend of the family since Maria-Teresa's mother took him in years before. Maria-Teresa is saddened and alarmed by the ominous behavior of Huascar and the Indians: word circulates that they have once again found an Inca king, and intend to celebrate the ancient rite of sacrificing a virgin bride to the Sun God.

Maria-Teresa is chosen as the bride and kidnapped by the Indians. Dick and the Marquis give chase, but to no avail until unexpectedly Huascar appears and promises to save Maria-Teresa. Knowing him to be in league with the Indians, Dick doesn't trust him but he has no choice. At last, by a stroke of luck an old madman leads Dick to the hidden sacrificial temple where they witness Maria-Teresa's entombment alive! Dick tries to save her and fails, but Huascar keeps his vow and saves them both, at the cost of his own life.

Lindsay, David. *Devil's Tor*. London: G. P. Putnam's Sons, 1932.

David Lindsay, author of the classic fantasy novels *A Voyage to Arcturus* and *The Haunted Woman*, wrote four other novels that qualify as fantasy. Of these, *Devil's Tor* is undeniably the best, and it is in many ways the crowning point of his career, the key to all of his creative work.

Hugh Drapier, a Highland Scot, is visiting Ingrid Fletcher, a distant relative. Drapier persuades the girl to take him up to Devil's Tor, an unusual rock formation that looks like some huge, thirty-foot-high head of a gargoyle or demon. As they gaze upon the grotesque statue, a flash of lightning strikes the rock, revealing an underground tomb beneath it.

Drapier descends into the enclosure, but stumbles and loses his light; then, the giant form of a beautiful woman appears on the stone table in the center of the tomb and slowly fades away. In the depths of the tomb, Hugh picks up a small stone that matches another in the possession of Ingrid. The smooth features of the stones contain depths that draw the viewer into another world, and Hugh is convinced that the two rocks somehow fit together and that their joining has some unfathomable occult significance. But Drapier is killed shortly thereafter by a rock which falls on the Tor, and he is replaced by Henry Saltfleet, who will complete the destiny of the stones. Both Saltfleet and Fletcher have had visions of prehistoric men and supernal women. The brooding shape of the Tor draws them to it on an evening filled with anticipation. In the chill of the night, the two halves of the stone are rejoined and the giant Demiurge appears for one last time. Then the spectacle fades, and Saltfleet and Ingrid are left to live out the separate broken remnants of their lives.

Linklater, Eric. *A Spell for Old Bones*. London: Jonathan Cape, 1949.

Eric Linklater, who is known for such gentle and sublime fantasies as "Sealskin Trousers," here provides a robust tale of Celtic myth and legend. In first-century Scotland lives a youth named Albyn, who decides to become a poet since he doesn't like to work very much. He never writes any poetry either, but he does become a good lover and manages to cure Liss, the king's daughter, of her speechlessness in a wholly unique and interesting way. The kingdom is actually run by Furbister, a lumpish giant who hates the world for what it has done to him, and who enjoys ruling without actually having to be king.

Many leagues away dwells another unhappy giant, Od McGammon, who has convinced himself that his oppression is actually beneficial for the people he is ruling. Both giants fear and suspect each other, and in addition Od is jealous of Furbister, since Albyn has managed to find him a wife of equal proportions. The end is inevitable: they meet with all their armies in mortal combat in a peat bog, and both the giants, the giant's wife, and most of their soldiers are killed in the struggle. The living body of Albyn is dug out from under the putrefying remains of Bala the giantess some days later, and the poet who never was a poet returns to dreaming about fame and the waiting arms of his lovely wife.

London, Jack. *Hearts of Three*. London: Mills & Boon, 1918.

The recent recognition of Jack London as a significant and impressive contributor to the literature of fantasy and science fiction has resulted in the reprinting of much of his work in these fields, including *The Scarlet Plague* and the SF short story "The Red One." However, one novel has remained unavailable and all but unknown, even to many who are familiar with London's science fiction. While far from a major work, it is nevertheless worthy of reprinting as it is a genuine lost-race novel, complete with hidden city, half-savage inhabitants, treasure, and a beautiful White Queen with clairvoyant powers! But unlike most writers of lost-race stories, London refuses to take the business seriously, and burlesques the whole thing in a fast-moving, often hilarious "anything-goes" piece of "frenzied fiction."

In 1915 the Hearst newspaper chain commissioned London to novelize a motion-picture serial scenario by Charles Goddard, author of such silent serial classics as *The Perils of Pauline* and *The Exploits of Elaine*. London completed the novelization of Goddard's fifteen chapters in 1916, not long before his death, and apparently enjoyed the unusual experience immensely. *Hearts of Three* was serialized in Hearst's New York *Evening Journal* in 1919, after book publication in England in 1918. Unfortunately, no film was ever made from it.

A restless young heir to millions, Frank Morgan, descendant of the famous pirate, goes to Panama to search for the pirate's legendary hidden treasure. There he meets a distant relative, Francis Morgan, and becomes immediately entangled in a series of wild, incredible, and often highly dangerous adventures which ultimately lead to the discovery of a lost city of Mayans and their mysterious White Queen, the Lady Who Dreams. The Morgans manage to escape the wrath of the Sun God and return to civilization with the Queen, where more complications of a romantic and financial nature ensue. A return expedition to the lost city brings more adventure, tragedy, and, finally—a happy ending.

London, Jack. *The Scarlet Plague.* New York: Macmillan, 1915.

In his finest science-fiction book, Jack London predicts a primitive, broken-down civilization in the twenty-first century, when mankind has been decimated by a terrible plague. Old Granser is the only man alive who can still remember what life was like before the plague. In those days, Granser recalls, he was known as Professor James Howard Smith of the University of California, and life in the comfortable, mechanized world seemed safe and secure. But then the plague came in the year 2013, and its terrible scourge, a scarlet rash that killed within an hour, leaving no defense.

As it spread, civilization rapidly disintegrates, and people everywhere revert to savagery. Riots, fires, and hideous atrocities were commonplace. Somehow Granser was spared, and he wandered for months, or perhaps years, searching for survivors, just managing to stay alive. Finally he came upon a small group of people who called themselves the Santa Rosa tribe.

And now, sixty years later, men are savages, and as Granser tells his story to the young boys, Edwin and Hoo-Hoo, he sees that it means nothing to them beyond entertainment. They tease and mock him when he rambles on about things they can't comprehend. But Granser continues to babble, grateful for an audience of any kind, as he states London's theme, that men will once again invent gunpowder and weapons to kill themselves by the millions, that civilization will flourish again briefly, and then fall and pass away.

Machen, Arthur. *The Children of the Pool and Other Stories*. London: Hutchinson, 1936.

There is no doubt that when the history of the supernatural story is written anew, Arthur Machen's name will occupy a prominent position. H. P. Lovecraft believed him to be one of the leading writers in the genre, saying, "The fact remains that his powerful horror-material...stands alone in its class, and marks a distinct epoch in the history of this literary form." This collection represents some of the best of Machen's later work.

"The Children of the Pool" torment Roberts into reliving a part of his life he'd rather forget. "The Exalted Omega" tells the story of Mrs. Ladislaw, a cheap medium whose special effects sometimes scare even her. "The Bright Boy" is actually a full-grown man who masquerades as a child to perpetrate his diabolical crimes upon unsuspecting women. In "The Tree of Life," Teilo Morgan, a hopeless invalid, runs his estate from his bed to keep himself amused; of course, his mansion is really an insane asylum. M'Calmont is well-known as a painter of landscapes, until he becomes obsessed with drawing the Twisted Man; his portraits become increasingly realistic, when one day the figure just steps "Out of the Picture." "Change" is the story of a diabolical cult discovered on the Welsh coast that warps the souls of innocent children.

Marryat, Florence. *The Dead Man's Message: An Occult Romance*. New York: Charles B. Reed, Publisher, 1894.

The supernatural tale as religious example was extremely common in the late nineteenth century. This book is typical of the lot.

Professor Henry Aldwyn is a learned scholar thoroughly despised by his family and friends. When the old man finally dies of a seizure one evening, he awakens next to his body, and finds himself unable to move away from it. He listens to the rejoicing of the servants and the harsh opinions of his "friends," and is beginning to rail against their collective ingratitude, when another spirit appears nearby.

John Forest has come to guide the ugly scientist through the afterlife, and he tells Henry that he must work to repair the damage caused during his life if he is to have any hopes of spending eternity in happiness. Aldwyn asks to see the soul of his first wife, but she turns away from him in disgust and shame, and tells him he is making his own hell. The only rectification available to the scientist is the redemption of the children he rejected while on Earth; he caused their souls to become warped, and now he must restore them to good spiritual health, or face the afterlife alone. After much travail, Henry finally sees the light, and begins the long road to spiritual purification by rescuing his son from a life of degradation on an old freighter. When he is finally capable of falling humbly to his knees, Aldwyn is left with his son to watch over his development, and John Forest returns to paradise, leaving the old man with the promise of redemption after much suffering and sacrifice

Marsh, Richard. *The Beetle: A Mystery.* London: Skeffington & Son, 1897.

Long regarded as a classic by horror buffs (Lovecraft called it a worthy successor to *Dracula*), *The Beetle* is the story of an ancient Egyptian cult of Isis which seeks to dominate naive young men, and sacrifice the helpless women who wander into its lair. Paul Lessingham was once such a victim, but he now believes he has overcome the spell cast by the Beetle. Soon after he announces his engagement to Marjorie Lindon, the strange, almost feminine figure of the Beetle reappears in London and seeks revenge upon his former adherent.

Robert Holt, a homeless beggar, becomes the creature's unwilling tool, and, like all who come in contact with the mystery, is horrified whenever the thing appears. Marjorie is kidnapped, and Paul is convinced the Beetle intends her to be his next sacrificial victim. His fears are enhanced when he discovers the body of Holt in a disreputable boarding house, where it apparently has been discarded when

Holt's usefulness had ended. The "Arab" is seen entering a train with Marjorie disguised as a beggar boy: Paul tries to overtake the Pullman, but is rapidly outdistanced.

Suddenly, he comes upon the wreck of the cars, apparently caused by an explosion in the Beetle's compartment. Marjorie's barely living body is huddled in a corner, nearly smothered in a gooey mess of blood or paint or life fluid from some large unknown animal (the scientists are unsure). Having been released from the creature's nefarious spell, Marjorie and Lessingham are free at last to return to their normal lives, and their wedding promises a bright future.

Marshall, Sidney J. *The King of Kor; or, She's Promise Kept: A Continuation of the Great Story of "She" of H. Rider Haggard.* Washington: S. J. Marshall, 1903.

The immediate success and popularity of H. Rider Haggard's classic fantasy novel *She* (1886) led to a host of parodies and imitations, some written by his friend and colleague Andrew Lang. But the book's impression on one author was so great that, unable to wait for the sequel that was inevitably to come, he wrote and published at his own expense a sequel of his own, in which Ayesha fulfills her promise to Leo Vincey and Horace Holly to return to them in all her beauty. *The King of Kor*, an extremely scarce book since its original publication, remains the only serious clothbound continuation of *She* ever published. As the author states in his foreword: "[*She*'s] characters impressed themselves so indelibly upon my mind that they have been constantly before me, almost as living companions, and each one seemed in fancy to implore me to pursue them and unfold a sequel of their existence and record their further experiences."

After hesitating for many years, the author finally produced this strange, unearthly sequel, ironically only two years before Haggard's own sequel *Ayesha: The Return of She*, was published! Although there are a few similarities, the two sequels are quite different in approach. Haggard employs reincarnation, magic, and other occult phenomena, but always balances it with a strong storyline and lots of action. In contrast, Marshall offers relatively little action, instead concentrating on extensions of Haggard's mystical philosophy.

Ayesha returns to Leo and Holly in spirit form, and guides them back to the lost kingdom of Kor, where Leo becomes king and rules in her place. She asks them to destroy her withered body, which still reposes in the cave of Living Fire, so that her tormented soul can be at peace at last. Having proved to them that "there is no death," she promises that Leo will soon die and join her in eternal love beyond death. He does and Holly chronicles the strange adventure, looking forward to his own death when he will join his spirit love also, a woman he met in the caves of Kor.

McHugh, Vincent. *I Am Thinking of My Darling: An Adventure Story*. New York: Simon & Schuster, 1943.

A strange plague has hit New York City. It dissolves the inhibitions of its victims like sugar in a cup of tea. The disease makes the patient do exactly what he or she wants to do, regardless of consequences. Hundreds of thousands of New Yorkers are seized simultaneously with this not-too-unpleasant malady. The city's economic life begins breaking down. Henpecked husbands suddenly find the courage to leave their wives. The mayor decides he hates his job and abdicates. Women who always wanted to flirt with men (or go further) suddenly do it. Jim Rowan, a New York City official, finds himself acting mayor of a city whirling around in the grip of some unknown epidemic. His actress wife, Niobe, has left him for what seems to be (to him) ridiculous reasons, and he is forced to start tracking her down, while simultaneously trying to cope with this strange plague of happiness. In the end, Niobe is found and the epidemic is conquered. Life returns to normal, if it ever can be normal again.

Menville, Douglas, and R. Reginald, editors. *Ancestral Voices: An Anthology of Early Science Fiction*. New York: Arno Press, 1975.

CONTENTS:

Bangs, John Kendrick. "A Glance Ahead; Being a Christmas Tale of A.D. 3568," from *Over the Plum Pudding.* New York: Harper & Bros., 1901.

Chambers, Robert W. "The Third Eye," from *Police!!!* New York: D. Appleton, 1915.

Cummins, Harle Oren. "The Space Annihilator," from *Welsh Rarebit Tales.* Boston: Mutual Book Co., 1902.

Griffith, George. "A Corner in Lightning," from *Gambles with Destiny.* London: F. V. White, 1899.

Hyne, C. J. Cutcliffe. "The Lizard," from *Atoms of Empire.* New York and London: Macmillan, 1904.

Lang, Andrew. "The Romance of the First Radical," from *The Wrong Paradise and Other Stories.* New York: Harper & Bros., 1887.

London, Jack. "The Red One," from *The Red One.* New York: Macmillan, 1918.

Robertson, Morgan. "Beyond the Spectrum," from from *The Wreck of the Titan; or, Futility.* New York: McClure's Magazine & Metropolitan Magazine, 1914.

Sullivan, James F. "Impossibility: A Study of Reason and Science," from *Queer Side Stories.* London: Downey & Co., 1900.

Waterloo, Stanley. "Love and a Triangle," from *The Wolf's Long Howl.* Chicago: H. S. Stone & Co., 1899.

These ten stories, originally published between 1886 and 1918, are illustrative of themes which have become standard topics in more recent science fiction. Andrew Lang, for example, provides a satirical prehistory in a humorous vein. Morgan Robertson's tale combines the future war theme with an advanced scientific invention. The author of *The Story of Ab*, Stanley Waterloo, confronts the problem of communicating with another planet. A bitingly satirical look at humanity's faith in science and reason is demonstrated in James F. Sullivan's "Impossibility." John Kendrick Bangs, well-known for his humorous ghost stories, gives us his own peculiar view of life in the far future, when the U.S. covers the entire Western hemisphere, and androids and interplanetary travel are commonplace.

Harle Oren Cummins tells of the invention of a matter transmitter. Cutcliffe Hyne, who wrote the classic novels

The Lost Continent and *Empire of the World*, brings to life a huge prehistoric reptile in an underground cavern. Robert W. Chambers, one of the most popular writers of his day, portrays a human mutation. Finally, in what must certainly rank as Jack London's finest science-fiction story, we learn of an alien object, perhaps a spaceship, which came to Earth thousands of years ago, and is still worshiped by savages as a god. His tale has particular relevance in light of the current speculation on possible visitations from outer space during prehistoric times.

Menville, Douglas and R. Reginald, editors. *Ancient Hauntings.* New York: Arno Press, 1976.
CONTENTS:
Blavatsky, H. P. "The Ensouled Violin," from *Nightmare Tales.* London: Theosophical Publishing House, 1892.
Campbell, Gilbert. "The Green Staircase," from *Dark Stories from the Sunny South; or, Legends of the Mediterranean.* London: Ward, Lock & Co., 1889.
Davies, Howell. "The Haunted Hansom," from *Stories with a Vengeance* (an anonymous anthology). London: John Dicks, 1870.
de la Motte Fouqué, Frédéric. "The Vial-Genie and Mad Farthing," a translation of "Das Galgenmännlein" from *Kleine Romane*, reprinted from *Miniature Romances from the German, with Other Profusions of Light Literature*, edited by Thomas Tracy. Boston: C. C. Little & J. Brown, 1841.
McNish, Robert. "The Metempsychosis," from *Famous Occult Tales*, edited by Frederick B. De Berard. New York: Isaac H. Blanchard, 1899.
Magherini-Graziani, Giovanni, translated by Mary A. Craig. "Fioraccio," from *Modern Ghosts* (an anonymous anthology). New York & London: Harper & Bros., 1890.
Rabe, Ann C., writing as Von Degen. "A Mystery of the Campagna," from *A Mystery of the Campagna and A Shadow on a Wave.* London: T. Fisher Unwin, 1891.
Sala, George Augustus. "The Green Hands: A Story About a Duet," from *Terrible Tales.* London: John Dicks, 1873.

Turgenev], Ivan. "Ghosts," from *Tales for a Stormy Night* (an anonymous anthology). Cincinnati: Robert Clarke, 1891.

The nine stories included in this anthology are representative of themes common to the early classical period of supernatural fiction (mid- and late nineteenth century). In "The Ensouled Violin," the famous mystic Madame Blavatsky tells the tale of Franz Stenio, who uses strings made from human intestines in a futile attempt to outplay the violin of Paganini. "The Green Staircase" is haunted by the souls of a man and his murdered wife, and the pair are forced to replay the tragedy every year on the anniversary of her death.

A horrible murder is solved when the spirit of the deceased appears in "The Haunted Hansom." In "A Mystery of the Campagna," a rare pre-Dracula tale, a centuries-old vampire ensnares a young Italian composer. Richard buys himself "The Vile-Genie and Mad Farthing," and finds the demon will give him all the money he needs in exchange for his soul if he dies with the fiend in his possession. "The Metempsychosis" tells the story of a man who makes a drunken agreement to exchange his soul with another, and finds to his horror that it is really happening. In "Fioraccio," a rascally Italian dies, but refuses to stay buried in consecrated ground. Virginia was practicing a song on the piano, when "The Green Hands" suddenly made it a duet. Ivan Turgenev tells the story of a mysterious and beautiful phantom who takes a young man on a series of astral voyages in space and time, in "Ghosts."

Menville, Douglas, and R. Reginald, editors. *Dreamers of Dreams: An Anthology of Fantasy*. New York: Arno Press, 1978.

CONTENTS:

Bangs, John Kendrick. "The Affliction of Baron Humpelhimmel," from *Over the Plum-Pudding*. New York: Harper & Bros., 1901.

Housman, Laurence. "The Blind God," from *Gods and Their Makers and Other Stories*. London: John Lane, 1897.

MacDonald, George. "The Gray Wolf," from *The Portent and Other Stories*. London: T. Fisher Unwin, 1909.

Stoker, Bram. "The Invisible Ghost," from *Under the Sunset*. London: Sampson Low, Marston, Searle & Rivington, 1882.

Boothby, Guy. "A Professor of Egyptology," from *The Lady of the Island*. London: John Long, 1904.

Lang, Andrew. "The End of Phaeacia," from *In the Wrong Paradise and Other Stories*. London: Kegan Paul, Trench & Co., 1886.

Morris, Kenneth. "The Last Adventure of Don Quixote," from *The Secret Mountain and Other Tales*. London: Faber & Gwyer, 1926.

Peake, Mervyn. "Same Time, Same Place," from *Science Fantasy* 20 (1963): 60.

Mitchell, J. A. "That First Affair," from *That First Affair and Other Sketches*. New York: Charles Scribner's Sons, 1902.

Hale, Edward Everett. "The Queen of California," from *His Level Best and Other Stories*. Boston: J. R. Osgood, 1873.

Arnold, Edwin Lester. "Rutherford the Twice-Born," from *The Story of Ulla*. London: Longmans, Green & Co., 1895.

Dunsany, Lord. "The Journey of the King," from *Time and the Gods*. London: William Heinemann, 1906.

Bates, H. E. *The Seekers*. London: John & Edward Bumpus, 1926.

In contrast to science-fiction writers, writers of fantasy seem to prefer the longer forms, the novel and the novella; much of the most notable work produced in the latter genre has been in these forms. The novels of such famed authors as William Morris, C. S. Lewis, E. R. Eddison, George MacDonald, and J. R. R. Tolkien, for example, are far better known than their shorter pieces. And yet, many excellent fantasy tales exist in short story and "novelette" form and deserve to become better known and appreciated. This anthology presents a sampling of such work, by authors both famous and less well known, the shorter visions—but no less rich—of these "dreamers of dreams."

Of special interest are two short lost-race stories, rarities in an area given almost exclusively to the novel. "The

End of Phaeacia" is a lost-race novelette dedicated to H. Rider Haggard and "She" by Haggard's close friend and sometime collaborator, Andrew Lang, yet published before *She!* It tells of the discovery in the South Seas of a lost civilization of ancient Greeks, the last remnant of Hellenic culture, and its destruction by modern man. "The Queen of California" is a retelling of what is probably the first lost-race fantasy ever written, from the *Sergas de esplandián*, published around 1510—the fantastic tale of Amadis of Gaul and Queen Calafia, who gave her name to California—a story rescued from oblivion by Edward Everett Hale, author of "The Man Without a Country."

Menville, Douglas and R. Reginald, editors. *Phantasmagoria.* New York: Arno Press, 1976.
CONTENTS:
Benson, E. F. "The Sanctuary," from *More Spook Stories.* London: Hutchinson, 1934.

Birkin, Charles Lloyd. "The Terror on Tobit," from *Devils' Spawn.* London: George Allan & Unwin, 1936.

Broster, D(orothy) K(athleen). "Couching at the Door," from *Couching at the Door.* London: William Heinemann, 1942.

Cabell, James Branch. "An Amateur Ghost," from *Argosy Magazine* 38:3 (February, 1902).

"The Closed Cabinet" (anonymously written), from *The Lock and Key Library: The Most Interesting Stories of All Nations; Old Time English*, edited by Julian Hawthorne. New York: Review of Reviews Co., 1915.

Doyle, Arthur Conan. "Playing with Fire," from *Round the Fire Stories.* New York: The McClure Company, 1908.

Garnett, Richard. "The Demon Pope," from *The Twilight of the Gods and Other Tales.* London: T. Fisher Unwin, 1888.

Gautier, Théophile. "Arria Marcella," translated by Lafcadio Hearn, from *One of Cleopatra's Nights and Other Fantastic Romances.* New York: R. Worthington, 1882.

Hall, Manly P. "The Witch Doctor," from *Shadow Forms: A Collection of Occult Stories.* Los Angeles: Hall Publishing Co., 1925.

John, Jasper. "The Seeker of Souls," from *Sinister Stories*. London: Henry Walker, 1930.

The Late Duke of Northumberland. "The Shadow on the Moor," from *Strange Tales from 'Blackwood'* (an anonymous anthology). Edinburgh & London: William Blackwood & Sons, 1950.

Pain, Barry. "The Moon-Slave," from *Ghosts and Marvels: A Selection of Uncanny Tales from Daniel Defoe to Algernon Blackwood*, edited by V. H. Collins. London: Humphrey Milford, Oxford University Press, 1924.

Pater, Roger. "A Porta Inferi," from *Mystic Voices: Being Experiences of the Rev. Philip Rivers, Pater Squire and Priest, 1834-1913)*. London: Burns, Oates & Washbourne, 1923.

In *Ancient Hauntings*, we presented a number of chilling tales from our nineteenth-century archives. This companion volume concentrates on the current century, with representative stories spanning thirty years in the history of the supernatural story from 1900 to 1930.

E. F. Benson's classic story, "The Sanctuary," tells how Francis Elton discovers a bizarre Satanic cult hidden away in his uncle's house. In "The Terror on Tobit," three friends scoff at the ridiculous superstitions associated with that island, and then suddenly find themselves running for their lives. "Couching at the Door" is the famous story of Augustine Marchant, who is haunted by the strange visitation of a woman's boa. Cabell tells how a young American, a guest in an English castle, is called upon by his ghostly ancestors to haunt the place for one night. The anonymous tale, "The Closed Cabinet," reveals an ancient curse which has plagued the Mervyns for centuries, until it is broken by a courageous woman.

In "Playing with Fire," an experiment with the other world turns a séance into a terrifying and dangerous experience. Richard Garnett tells the amusingly irreverent tale of what happens when the devil becomes pope. In "Arria Marcella," a young man's love for a long-dead lady of Pompeii enables her to transport him back through time. Gomo, "The Witch Doctor," cannot fight the fire sticks of the white man with his primitive arrows, but the invaders had not expected to face the terrible weapons of nature. Jasper John tells of a haunted room in an old castle which harbors a malignant horror that drives men to madness and suicide. Northumberland relates how "The Shadow on the Moor" exacts a fearful vengeance on a murderer. In "The Moon-Slave," the innocent moonlight dancing of a princess becomes a thing of horror. "A Porta Inferi" is the story of a man who dabbles in spiritualism, becoming possessed by an evil spirit which is exorcised many years later.

Menville, Douglas, and R. Reginald, editors. *Worlds of Never: Three Fantastic Novels*. New York: Arno Press, 1978.

CONTENTS:

Bangs, John Kendrick. *Alice in Blunderland: An Iridescent Dream*. New York: Doubleday, Page, 1907.

Peacock, Lucy. *The Adventures of the Six Princesses of Babylon in Their Travels to the Temple of Virtue: An Allegory*. London: T. Bensley, 1785.

Taylor, Bert Leston, and W. C. Gibson. *The Log of the Water Wagon; or, The Cruise of the Good Ship "Lithia."* Boston: H. M. Caldwell, 1905.

These three fantasy novels are reprinted in one volume for the first time. *Alice in Blunderland* is one of Bangs's scarcest works, a humorous sequel to *Alice in Wonderland* in which Alice finds herself back with her old friends, the Mad Hatter, the March Hare, and the White Knight. This time she is conducted on a tour through Blunderland, a "model city" founded by the Hatter, "where everything goes just right." Bangs proceeds to satirize unmercifully the absurdities and stupidities of modern municipal government and the practices of big business.

Lucy Peacock's novel, originally published anonymously, is a fantastic allegory filled with dwarfs, goblins, fairies, giants, and all the paraphernalia of the classic imaginative tale. In olden days reigned a certain King and Queen of Babylon renowned for their justice and mercy. But Babylon is defeated by a neighboring land, and the Queen and her six daughters take refuge in a nearby desert. The fairy Benigna appears, moved by their suffering, and transports the girls to the father's hiding-place on an island. The princesses are told to find six wonders of nature: the Distaff of Industry, a Bottle of Water from the River of Good Nature, the Spear of Truth, the Mantle of Meekness, the Magnet of True Generosity, and the White Wand of Contentment. How they succeed, and the adventures they share in the quest are the subjects of the quaint little tale.

"The Log of the Water Wagon" was found floating in a stoppered-up milk bottle, and it develops into a comical tale of the adventures of the good ship "Lithia," her passengers and crew. The writer of the log (selected by virtue of his being "the only sober passenger aboard") weaves an entertaining tapestry of incidents and anecdotes revolving around this frolicsome but ill-fated voyage. What *really* became of the passengers aboard the "Lithia"?

Merritt, A. *The Fox Woman & Other Stories*. New York: Avon Books, 1949.

A. Merritt, who died in 1943 at the age of fifty-nine, wrote a series of novels that have remained popular to this day. Books such as *The Metal Monster*, *The Moon Pool*, *Seven Footprints to Satan*, and *Dwellers in the Mirage* have ensured Merritt a place in the history of lost-race and fantasy literature. Less known are his handful of short stories, which were collected by Donald A. Wollheim during the latter's tenure as editor of Avon Books, and published in a slim paperback that saw just one printing before disappearing into oblivion.

Among the stories included in this virtually unobtainable volume are "The Fox Woman," the novelette which Hannes Bok later expanded into a book called *The Fox Woman and The Blue Pagoda*; "The People of the Pit," the classic story of an unnamable horror and the ruins of a lost civilization; "Through the Dragon Glass," a fantasy of Oriental magic and mystery; "Three Lines of Old French," in which a soldier in the trenches falls in love with a French girl 200 years old; and "The Drone," "The Last Poet and the Robots," "The White Road," "When Old Gods Wake," and "The Women of the Wood."

Merritt, A., and Hannes Bok. *The Fox Woman and the Blue Pagoda; The Black Wheel*. New York: Arno Press, 1976.

When Abraham Merritt died in 1943, he left behind a legacy of eight novels and about the same number of short stories, which together comprise some of the finest fantastic fiction ever written—and some of the most popular. After initial serialization in the pulps, most of the novels were issued first in hardcover and then reprinted in paperback editions. Merritt had begun work on two other novels which were left incomplete at his death. Hannes Bok, the well-known science-fiction illustrator, completed the two books, and decorated them with his own unique drawings for publication in two very limited editions issued by the New Collectors Group.

The first of the novels, *The Fox Woman*, consisted of about 15,000 words when Merritt laid it aside. Bok's long addition, *The Blue Pagoda*, brings to a thrilling climax the vengeful tale of Yin Hu, the beautiful and diabolical fox woman, a villainess in the best Merritt tradition. The second book, *The Black Wheel*, includes seven chapters started by Merritt, and concerns a pleasure cruise which gradually turns into a nightmare, as the passengers discover they are being possessed by the spirits of the dead. This is the first time these two scarce books have been published in one volume.

Mitchell, John Ames. *Drowsy*. New York: Frederick A. Stokes, 1917.

In an early example of the superman theme, Mitchell tells the story of an extraordinary boy named Cyrus Alton. Nicknamed "Drowsy" because of his languid expression, Cyrus displays a keen and inquiring mind, and also possesses a strange talent for reading the thoughts of others. He grows to manhood in a quiet New England town, and is soon able to exchange psychic messages with his childhood sweetheart, Ruth Heywood, over long distances. But Ruth's father is a missionary, and one day he leaves for China with his daughter.

Heartbroken, Cyrus plunges into his college studies, taking a particular interest in physics. His tremendous intellect and driving ambition lead to an astonishing series of discoveries and inventions, including an unlimited source of electricity, an anti-gravity machine, and a space ship which can travel to the planets. He journeys secretly to the Moon, where he finds the remains of a long-dead civilization, ruins millions of years old, and an immense diamond. The sale of the jewel makes him a wealthy man, and he returns to Earth to search for his long-lost love. But Ruth has entered a convent, and refuses his overtures. In desperation, he decides to make a final space voyage to Mars, from whence he will never return, but as he reaches the planet, Ruth's telepathic call reasserts her love for the inventor, and he joyously returns home.

Molesworth, Mrs. (Mary Louisa Stewart). *Uncanny Tales.* London: Hutchinson, 1896.

The most important story in this collection, "The Shadow in the Moonlight," tells of the strange haunting of Finster St. Mabyn's, where Leila's family has come for a summer holiday. Not long after they arrive, the girl's younger brother, Dormer, comes to her with the story of an odd visitation in the Gallery. Leila scoffs at the notion, but follows him down to allay his fears. Then, in the moonlight streaming through the window, she sees a shadow creeping along the edge of the room, with two bony-looking hands, and a head that seems too large for its body. The thing feels its way around and around the walls of the room, stopping briefly to fumble at the doors; as it passes over them they both experience a breath of icy air that's almost unbearable in its intensity.

Gradually the entire household becomes aware of their strange guest, and after a few more weeks the family moves on to a rectory temporarily left vacant by some friends. But they're shocked to find that the ghost has followed them to their new abode, and when they return to their own home, the spirit is still there, blindly moving around the room where they've hung a tapestry bought originally to decorate the Gallery of Finster St. Mabyn's.

It's Leila who has the idea: the ghost must haunt the tapestry! Her brother Phil does some checking, and discovers that the original owner had taken it from a room that had been walled off for over a hundred years. The tapestry room had had the reputation of being haunted by an ancestor who had robbed an acquaintance of a valuable ring during a card game. Phil searches the place, and finds a small alcove on the wall where the tapestry had originally been hung; inside is the ring itself wrapped in chamois. The ring is sold for charity, and the ghost walks no more. Other stories included are: "The Man with the Cough," "'—Will Not Take Place,'" "The Clock That Struck Thirteen," "'Halfway Between the Stiles,'" and "At the Dip of the Road."

Morris, Kenneth. *Book of the Three Dragons*. New York: Longmans, Green, 1930.

Like Greek and Irish mythology, Welsh mythology has provided a wealth of inspiration for writers of fantasy. Its influence can be clearly seen in the works of such authors as Lord Dunsany, E. R. Eddison, Robert E. Howard, Leigh Brackett, and J. R. R. Tolkien; direct recreations of Welsh myth have also been written with great effectiveness by Evangeline Walton, Katherine Kurtz, Lloyd Alexander, and Kenneth Morris, the least known of any of the authors mentioned, but probably the finest stylist of the lot, save only Dunsany and Eddison. Little is known of Morris except his publications: *The Fates of the Princes of Dyfed* (1914), published under the Welsh form of his name, "Cenydd Morus," *The Secret Mountain and Other Tales* (1926), and the present volume, his last. Of this latter work, Ursula K. Le Guin has written: "It is a singularly fine example of the recreation of a work magnificent in its own right (*The Mabinogion*)—a literary event rather rare except in fantasy, where its frequency is perhaps proof, if one were needed, of the ever-renewed vitality of myth."

The Fates of the Princes of Dyfed is based on the First Branch of the *Mabinogi*, and *Book of the Three Dragons* is a sequel, continuing a branch of the other long tale, but with some changes, adaptations from other branches, and much of the author's own invention. Man-awyddan and his six companions are bringing the living, bodiless head of Bran the Blessed to London to be crowned King, but the two talismans set in the castle of Gwalas by the Gods to protect the Seven are stolen by two thieves, stripping the two Gods of their power. The Seven sadly bury the Head and separate, and Man-awyddan goes forth on an epic quest to recover the talismans, fighting enchantments on earth and in the Underworld. At last, after battling three dragons, he achieves the power to retrieve the stolen charms. He then frees the enchanted armies, kings, and bards, who had turned to stone and were being held captive in the Underworld.

Morris, Ralph. *The Life and Astonishing Adventures of John Daniel*. London: M. Cooper, 1751.

This early imaginary voyage can be divided into two separate sections. John Daniel, son of an English smith, leaves his home over a family dispute, obtaining passage on a ship to China. The vessel is wrecked near the Malaccas by a violent storm, and John and one other crewman, Peter Thomas, are cast onto a small, uninhabited island. After great travail, they manage to find food and water, and build a small shelter on the island's single mountain. Thomas is injured falling from a tree, and refuses to allow John to examine him. John discovers that "Thomas" is really a woman named Ruth Cornins, who took passage on the ship to search for her lover. The two Britons decide to marry, and begin raising a family. After many years, all but one of their eleven children have intermarried in their turn, and settled on various parts of the island. The lone bachelor, Jacob Daniel, is a smith like his father, and prefers to spend his time making life easier for the islanders. He invents a flying machine, and invites his father to accompany him on a trial flight.

The second part of the book describes their joint adventures. Not realizing the power of the craft, they fly so high that the island is lost in the distance, and darkness falls before they can find their way back. With no way of landing at night, they continue to stay aloft, and finally find themselves descending into rugged mountains inhabited by curious, copper-colored beings all covered with hair. After an extraordinarily long night, the two voyagers manage to catch one of the timid natives, and request food and water with signs. But the nourishment is strangely unsatisfying, and the pair takes off once again. After a second lengthy flight, accompanied by strange phenomena, they reach a barren island, and are rescued by the monstrous offspring of a woman and a sea creature. The head of this bizarre clan is well educated, and upon hearing their story, tells the travelers they have visited the Moon. Daniel and his son finally reach Europe, where Jacob is killed on the way home to England. Several years later, John dies at the age of ninety-seven. Although published at about the same time as *Peter Wilkins,* this appears to be an independent story, and Daniel's flying machine is much more mechanically oriented than that of Wilkins.

Murray, G. G. A. *Gobi or Shamo: A Story of Three Songs.* London: Longmans, Green, 1889.

Mavrones has discovered a manuscript in an old Greek monastery that tells of a race of Greeks stranded for hundreds of years in the Gobi desert. Determined to find the truth of the tale, he organizes an expedition and obtains permission from the Imperial Chinese Government to penetrate the interior. In the midst of the wastes, they come upon a lake and a mountain fastness, and follow the course of a stream through a long and winding gorge. They are nearly precipitated over a waterfall, but are snatched at the last minute from destruction by an Englishman, Trench, who rules over a barbarian race called the Sanni.

From Trench, the party learns that the Hellenes do indeed exist and lead lives of leisure in their utopian city farther down the valley. The Sanni revolt and try to overthrow their king, but are destroyed by the powerful Greek explosives they have stolen. The Hellenes, startled to find their world penetrated again by outsiders (Trench had been the first in over a thousand years), hold a council and decide to let the explorers leave. The outer rocks of their citadel will then be electrified to prevent any unwarranted intrusions in the future. After many hardships, the Europeans find their way through the wilds of the Gobi, across the Chinese plains, and then through the mountains and barbarians of Tibet until they finally reach the civilized lands of British India. This novel is typical of the early lost-race tale, which used little-known areas of the world as hiding places for remnants of strange and ancient civilizations.

Newcomb, Simon. *His Wisdom, the Defender: A Story.* New York: Harper & Bros., 1940.

A future historian recounts the world-shaking events of the 1940s which led to the abolition of war, and the establishment of the most honored position in history, Defender of the Peace of the World. Professor Campbell, a brilliant Harvard instructor of molecular physics, discovers an anti-gravity substance called "etherine," and a "thermic" engine that can move automobiles, motorbikes, and airships on very little fuel. He resigns from the university, and develops a grand plan for bringing peace and prosperity to a suffering world on the verge of war.

Two mysterious citadels are established; one, called Campbelltown, is located on an island in the Potomac River, and the second, Uraniberg, is located on Elba. Recruiting a large number of young athletes, Campbell initiates them into the "Angelic Order of Seraphim," and trains them in the use of various advanced weapons, including flying mechanical men (individual tanks), incredibly fast submarines and flying contraptions, and strange, claw-armed metal centipedes.

Campbell orders the nations of the world to disarm voluntarily, and when they refuse, his submarines sink the navies of the world, his mechanical men capture thousands of troops, and everywhere opposition is destroyed. Germany capitulates when the Kaiser is taken prisoner, and one by one the other nations follow. A new era of peace and prosperity dawns under the leadership of "His Wisdom, the Defender," who was once damned by every civilized country, but now is acknowledged as mankind's greatest benefactor. Newcomb, a well-known astronomer of his time, died nine years after this novel was published.

O'Donnell, Elliott. *The Sorcery Club.* London: William Rider & Son, 1912.

Better known for his accounts of "true" supernatural manifestations, Elliott O'Donnell produced several novels of occult horror early in his career. In the best known of these,

The Sorcery Club, he shows the terrible consequences of the misuse of ancient occult powers by a group of greedy young men. Leon Hamar, an unemployed clerk in San Francisco, buys an old book in a second-hand bookshop. Together with two other unemployed friends, Matt Kelson and Ed Curtis, he examines the tome and discovers it to be a record of the voyages of a sailor named Thomas Maitland, printed in 1693. Maitland was shipwrecked on an island off the coast of Ireland, where he discovered an ancient chest containing manuscripts from Atlantis.

The manuscript relates the story of the destruction of Atlantis, and contained formulae for all kinds of sorcery and black magic, originated by the Atlanteans. At first incredulous. the three friends decide to try the incantations, which give step-by-step directions for attaining various kinds of occult power. They succeed in passing the required tests, despite several blood-curdling occult manifestations, and summon up an evil spirit called "The Unknown," who initiates them into the secrets of the Atlantean Black Arts. The three men form a group called "The Sorcery Club" and proceed to use their new powers to obtain wealth, ruin their enemies, and compel the love of women who despise them. But their selfish machinations cause them to quarrel among themselves, thereby breaking the harmony of the group and ending their power over others. The horrible forces of the "Unknown," who had warned them of the consequences of disharmony, now come to claim them.

Onions, Oliver. *Widdershins*. London: Martin Secker, 1911.

Oliver Onions is little remembered today except for his extraordinary ghost stories, the best of which appeared in this first collection. Indeed, Peter Penzoldt, author of *The Supernatural in Fiction*, regards "The Beckoning Fair One," the initial story in the book, as "among the finest short stories of the supernatural ever written." He goes on to say:

> "The Beckoning Fair One," like Blackwood's "The Damned," is the story of an invisible presence—the ghost, or spirit of a

person or persons, whose intense personality allowed the psychic part of their being to continue after death, and exert an evil influence. In both stories the presence of the ghost or spirit is felt rather than actually perceived by the senses. The theme is the spell that a house may exercise over a sensitive temperament. But the difference between the two is appreciated when attention is focused on the principal actors. Mr. Onions's tale is about a young man, who, living alone in the haunted house, falls in love with the invisible presence of a woman. This unnatural love first leads him to forsake his living girlfriend, and then, by degrees, to give up work, lose all interest in life, and finally almost to die of starvation, without noticing he was doing so. Only the noise of a woman combing her hair and the persistent melody sung by the drops falling from a water-tap indicate the invisible presence in the house....

Also included in this volume are: "Phantas," "Rooum," "Benlian," "Io," "The Accident," "The Cigarette Case," "The Rocker," and "Hic Jacet."

Owen, Frank. *The Purple Sea: More Splashes of Chinese Color*. New York: Lantern Press, 1930.

A curious subgenre of fantasy fiction is the pseudo-Oriental tale as exemplified by the Kai Lung stories of Ernest Bramah. Both Bramah and Frank Owen, who also specialized in this kind of writing, created a never-never land ostensibly laid in China, but bearing as much relation to that country as China does to Africa. These are gentle fantasies, filled with the charm of Oriental wisdom, exotic scenery and touches of the supernatural. Among the stories included in this collection are: "The Golden Hour of Kwoh Fan," "The Purple Sea," "The Silent Trees," "The Lantern-Maker," "Gobi Interlude," "The Perfumes of Chow Wan," "The Quaint Manuscript of Wu Wang," "The Rice Merchant,"

"Love Letters of a Little House," "The Tinkle of the Camel's Bell," and "The Old Man Who Swept the Sky."

Pain, Barry. *Robinson Crusoe's Return.* London: Hodder & Stoughton, 1906.

The famous Crusoe, who has spent at least three hundred years on his desert island after finding the Methuselah plant, finally decides to leave his little realm, and sets sail on a makeshift raft, taking only his gun, a parrot, and provisions. After some months he is cast ashore on the British Isles, but finds modern civilization eminently perplexing. He can't understand, for example, why a young bather seems so disturbed when he borrows a few pieces of clothing. And the man with the food cart, why was he so upset when Robinson accepted his offer of fresh provisions? Are not these all God-given gifts? A stranger named "George Rats" attempts to enlighten the poor fellow, and offers to educate him in the ways of modern living in return for the worthless pieces of gold Crusoe carries around with him on his belt. The good seaman, who considers the booty the least valuable part of his gear, is only too happy to oblige, and soon finds himself with both the gold and Rats vanished.

Crusoe then sets out to find himself an occupation to restore his fortunes, but the poor sailor is obviously unsuited for most useful jobs. A showman finally offers him a post as a sideshow wild man, and for a moment it appears that he's finally found his niche. Unfortunately, he embraces a strange woman who looks like his ex-fiancée of three hundred years before, and is promptly beaten up by her husband. Wandering around in despair, he finds George Rats once again, and the thief uses Crusoe to unwittingly embezzle a large sum of money. When Robinson finally figures out what's going on, he decides that he just can't cope with the present century, and returns to the beach, where his belongings are still stashed away in a sea cave. With his faithful parrot in hand, he pushes his raft into the waves, and sets out once again to return to the civilized paradise of his secluded island.

Paine, Albert Bigelow. *The Great White Way: A Record of an Unusual Voyage of Discovery, and Some Romantic Love*

Affairs Amid Strange Surroundings. New York: J. F. Taylor, 1901.

Nicholas Chase, a young man who dreams of discovering a warm land in the Antarctic, persuades millionaire Chauncey Gale to finance an expedition to the South Pole. Accompanying the explorers are Gale's spirited daughter, Edith, Ferratoni, a young Italian scientist interested in psychic communication, and Sturritt, the ship's steward, an inventor of condensed food tablets. Gale's specially-equipped ship survives many dangers from the elements, and the party finally reaches an immense ice barrier thousands of feet high. Chase, Edith, Ferratoni, and several other members of the expedition sail over the ice wall in a balloon, and journey inland on a combination iceboat and sleigh. They sight many unknown animals, and continue onward until the snow and ice gradually disappear, and are replaced by vast fields of strange purple flowers.

The travelers are greeted by a graceful, gentle race of people similar in appearance to Orientals. Their peaceful kingdom is called the Land of the Sloping Sun. The lovely young Princess of the Lilied Hills shows the visitors the marvels of this utopia, including telepathic communication, the scientific proof of life after death, and a civilization that is totally opposed to materialism and technological development. When Chauncey Gale brashly proposes to remake their land with modern technology and machines, the people angrily rise up against the explorers, and all are forced to flee for their lives except Ferratoni, who is pardoned by the Princess, and remains to marry her. The others regain the safety of their ship and head for home, discovering a shipwrecked mariner and a vast hoard of gold on the return voyage.

Paine, the noted biographer of Mark Twain, used *The Great White Way* as an attack upon materialism and the expansion of scientific development at the expense of human values.

Paine, Albert Bigelow. *The Mystery of Evelin Delorme: A Hypnotic Story.* Boston: Arena Publishing, 1894.

Before the advent of Sigmund Freud, psychology was an undeveloped science, and hypnotism was regarded by many as an occult science that had strange and inexplicable effects on the human soul. Paine's novel anticipates much of Freud's work on schizophrenia. Julian Paul Goetze is a young St. Louis painter whose fame has already spread throughout the land. One day an extraordinarily beautiful woman walks into his studio, and requests a sitting. Goetze is captivated by her gentle smile, and asks Eva Delorme to return again as soon as possible. The painter is also seeing another girl, Evelin March, whose personality seems exactly opposite Eva's; where Delorme is kind and gentle, March is hard, tough, and uncompromising.

Goetze finds himself torn between the two women, and dreads the possibility of them accidentally meeting each other in his studio. He notes a certain resemblance in features, but is unable in his comparison of the two portraits to decide exactly what it is that the two girls share in common. One night his despair over the situation drives him to drink, and he takes the first train he can find out of town. During his absence, Evelin March enters his studio, and decides to lie in wait for her rival, whose portrait she has found. She spies the young girl just down the hall, and rushes towards her with knife upraised. But the blade of the stiletto ricochets off the mirror, and buries itself in her chest. And Paul Goetze, who has just leaped through the door, sees the cold, beautiful features of Evelin March suddenly melt away into the saintly loveliness of Eva Delorme.

Phillpotts, Eden. *A Deal with the Devil.* London: Bliss, Sands & Foster, 1895.

Mr. Daniel Dolphin comes down to breakfast on his hundredth birthday with a strange tale to tell. The previous night the devil had come to him in a dream, and announced that his allotted span of life had run its course. However, the demon offered a bargain deal: sign on the dotted line (in blood, of course), and old Daniel can have another ten years of life. What's more, since a man of a hundred years can scarcely get any pleasure out of life, Dolphin will grow younger during the period at the rate of ten years for every one that elapses. Daniel accepts, and the next morning finds a red mark on his shoulder where the demon had jabbed his pen for ink.

During the succeeding days, Dolphin begins showing a few signs of vigor, and then turns up the signed deed stashed away in a cupboard. His hair starts coming back, and he takes an interest once again in the ladies of the town. He proposes to a pleasant widow of seventy, then jilts her as he grows younger, and repeats the process several more times with increasingly younger women. The younger he becomes the more trouble he causes for Martha Dolphin, the spinster granddaughter who had taken care of the old man throughout his later life. Their relationship changes to fit the circumstances, from grandfather to father to brother to nephew to son to grandson, and the pair are forced to move constantly, being chased by relatives of the girls he seduces along the way.

But the end comes rapidly, and Grandfather gradually dwindles into childhood, and then assumes baby form. On midnight of the final day, the cries of an infant change suddenly into "Martha, Martha," and the old lady sees an ancient, bent figure of a man stretching out his bony fingers towards her. Something formless and unutterably evil comes between them, and the body disappears with a harsh laugh and the echo of a moan. The contract is fulfilled.

Potter, Margaret Horton. *Istar of Babylon: A Phantasy.* New York: Harper & Bros., 1902.

One of the most skillful blending of mythic supernaturalism and historical reality, *Istar of Babylon* is an epic novel of great scope and depth. The author brings to life the ancient world of Babylon under the rule of Nabonidus, grandson of Nebuchadrezzar and last native king of the Great City; through her talents characters who have always been merely strange-sounding names in ancient history texts become living, breathing personae, loving and hating with great passions as they enact their inevitable roles in the awful drama of the mortality of a goddess and the fall of Babylon.

The goddess Istar, daughter of the moon-god Sin, doubts the mercy of God in relation to man; for punishment she is banished to the earth, incarnate as a living goddess in

Babylon where she must remain until she finds man's true relation to God. A Greek shepherd-poet, Charmides, hears of the living Istar and journeys to Babylon to worship her. After a long and arduous trip which almost results in his death, Charmides reaches the Great City and beholds the goddess, incredibly beautiful and radiant with a silvery aura of power, worshipped by the people with great reverence. She bids him to go and live with a poor widow and her two daughters, Baba and Ramfia, and he finds himself immediately caught up in the intrigues of Babylonian politics.

The high priest Amraphel plots with the Jewish prophet Daniel, out of court favor since the death of Nebuchadrezzar, in order to wrest the throne from Nabonidus and his young son, Prince Belshazzar, who has fallen totally in love with Istar. She abandons her godhood for him and experiences the agonies of mortality, bearing him a son and losing her status as a goddess. Charmides, now married to Ramfia, never wavers in his loyalty to Istar and saves her life during the final siege and destruction of Babylon by Cyrus of Persia. Finally, her strength and beauty gone, Istar is permitted to die and rejoin her fellow gods in Heaven.

Powys, John Cowper. *Morwyn; or, The Vengeance of God*. London: Cassell, 1937.

This is a good example of the novel as propaganda. The narrator, a retired Captain in the British Army, loves a young Welsh girl named Morwyn. One day while walking in the hills with the girl's father (a famous vivisectionist), the couple is jolted by the impact of a huge meteor on the mountaintop. Miraculously, only the father is killed, and when the lovers finally awaken, they find themselves deep inside the earth, buried within an apparently unending series of passageways. The spirit of the father suddenly appears, and from out of the caverns more spirits arrive to escort the newly dead through this peculiar version of Hell. Here sadists and vivisectionists spend eternity watching giant television screens showing ruthless experimenters torturing the bodies of living animals. The only free spirit wandering amidst the crowds of shouting souls is Taliesin, an ancient

Welsh bard who has traveled through every part of the after-life searching for his old friend, Merlin.

The poet befriends the two humans, and saves them when the fiends of the caverns decide to torture the intruders by superimposing their spirits over the earthly flesh. Down into an immense open pit flies the Welshman's craft, pursued by thousands of screaming ghosts. Finally they reach the great inner sea, and an island where they find the entrance to the Cauldron of Annwn. Still tormented by the evil beings from above, the beleaguered humans locate the sleeping body of Merlin, who vanquishes the vivisectionists by inflicting upon them the horrors they have perpetrated on the helpless experimental animals. Then Socrates wanders out of the mists, and together with Rhadamanthus, Judge of the Golden Age, they seek out the last of the Titans, the giant Tityos, whom they rescue from eternal torment. Just beyond the body of the god-man are two great stairwells stretching into the sky, and Socrates carries the injured officer up the right-hand path, homeward bound once again.

Praed, Mrs. Campbell (Rosa Caroline Murray-Prior). *The Brother of the Shadow: A Mystery of To-Day.* London: George Routledge & Sons, 1886.

Julian Vascher has sent his wife, Antonia, who is suffering from unbearable migraine headaches, to his old friend Dr. Lemuel Lloyd, a renowned practitioner of electrical magnetism and mesmerism. Lloyd has studied the works of the great spiritualists of the Orient, and his desire for learning the mysteries of the occult world has led him to the writings of obscure mystics and magicians. Staying with him on the Riviera is the Hindu ascetic Ananda, the pupil of certain adepts in India, with whom Ananda is able to communicate through astral projection and psychological telegraphy. Dr. Lloyd is immediately struck by Antonia's beauty, and is moved by pity and love to relieve her unceasing pain. His treatments seem to have a soothing effect upon the beautiful girl, and they gradually become fond of each other.

Lloyd is astonished to find that Toni has a sensitivity to psychic influences; while mesmerized she describes the coast of Egypt (which she has never seen), and a dark-skinned man in a red turban beckoning to her. Ananda tells Lemuel that the figure is the high priest of a black magic cult, and that the danger to the girl is very great. But the figure of the priest appears to Lloyd himself, and tempts him with knowledge he is unable to gain through his own meager efforts. The doctor wants the girl for himself, so he decides to use the occult powers offered by the magician to kill her husband. He materializes the Scin-Lecca, or astral double, of Julian Vascher, in order to murder him at a distance. Ananda calls for the aid of his White Adept, and Antonia renounces Lloyd's advances; the Scin-Lecca, now out of control, turns on the initiate in revenge, and the doctor is destroyed by his own desires.

Reginald, R., and Douglas Menville, editors. *King Solomon's Children: Some Parodies of H. Rider Haggard.* New York: Arno Press, 1978.

CONTENTS:

Biron, Henry Chartres, writing as Hyder Ragged. *King Solomon's Wives; or, The Phantom Mines.* London: Vizetelly & Co., 1887

De Morgan, John, writing as "the Author of 'He,' 'It,' 'Pa,' 'Ma,' etc." *King Solomon's Treasures.* New York: Norman L. Munro, 1887.

De Morgan, John, writing as "the Author of 'King Solomon's Wives,' 'King Solomon's Treasures,' 'He,' 'It,' etc., etc." *Bess: A Companion to "Jess."* New York: Norman L. Munro, 1887.

The history of popular literature was changed the day that Henry Rider Haggard, an obscure novelist, bet his brother that he could do better than Robert Louis Stevenson. The result was *King Solomon's Mines*, the book that made Haggard's literary reputation and established him as a best-selling writer. An indication of its popularity is the fact that the novel has never been out of print since it was published in 1885. If parody is the sincerest form of flattery, then Haggard was indeed flattered during his lifetime by the appearance of no less than nine parodies and one sequel, *The King of Kor*.

Haggard's parodies have always been difficult to trace, having been produced in cheap paperback editions that have barely survived the ages, under a variety of pseudonyms (or anonymously), with numerous changes in imprints. The three novels included in this volume represent two of the three known parodies of *King Solomon's Mines*, and the one parody of Haggard's historical novel *Jess*. This is the first time these exceedingly rare novels have been reprinted in one volume.

Reginald, R. and Douglas Menville, editors. *R.I.P.: Five Stories of the Supernatural*. New York: Arno Press, 1976.

CONTENTS:

Barker, Granville. *Souls on Fifth*. Boston: Little, Brown & Co., 1917.

Billings, Maris Herrington. *An Egyptian Love Spell*. New York: Central Publishing Co., 1914.

Kelland, Clarence Budington. *Thirty Pieces of Silver*. New York & London: Harper & Bros., 1913.

Lafargue, Paul, translated by Charles H. Kerr. *The Sale of an Appetite*. Chicago: Charles H. Kerr, 1904.

Oxenham, John. *The Cedar Box*. London: Longmans, Green, 1924.

Our first anthology of pamphlets, *The Spectre Bridegroom and Other Horrors*, offered a variety of supernatural thrills from the nineteenth century. In this companion volume, we concentrate on the tormented souls of more recent times.

In "An Egyptian Love Spell," Jack Drummond buys an ancient scarab ring in a jewelry store, and after putting the artifact on his finger, finds himself reliving his earlier existence as an Assyrian officer; when he returns to the real world, Drummond meets the reincarnated soul of the woman he loved three thousand years earlier, and is reunited once again with his destined bride.

"The Cedar Box" was fashioned by the boy Jesus during his days as an apprentice carpenter; miraculously, it survives in the modern world, and transforms the lives of all who come in contact with it, giving them the strength to continue.

Emile Bestouches is poor and hungry, and seems ready to commit suicide, when a rich glutton offers him $10,000 a month for "The Sale of an Appetite"; Destouches readily agrees, and then finds himself ruthlessly used as a digesting machine for the old man's obscene mastication.

Carnavon is a numismatist, and one day he receives a curious silver coin dating back to biblical times; while gazing on the inscription, he suddenly finds himself witnessing the salient points in the life of Judas Iscariot, and sees him betray the Christ with "Thirty Pieces of Silver"; when the vision ends, Carnavon gazes with awe on the coin he holds in his hand, and resolves to change his life.

The souls of the dead crowd the streets of New York, little puffs of flotsam and jetsam being blown here and there by the wind; the narrator discovers these "Souls on Fifth Avenue" and begins talking with them, seeking to learn their life stories; one girl in particular touches his heart, and to save her from an endless wandering in the streets of the city, he crushes her soul against his breast, and absorbs her essence into himself.

Reginald, R. and Douglas Menville, editors. *The Spectre Bridegroom and Other Horrors.* New York: Arno Press, 1976.

CONTENTS:

Alexa. *The Spectre Bridegroom: A Terrific and Interesting Tale.* London: Dean & Munday, 1880?

Anonymous. *The Demon Hunter; or, The White Wolf of the Hartz Mountains.* London?: 1850.

Maistre, Xavier de, translated by Edmund Goldsmid. *A Nocturnal Expedition Round My Room.* Edinburgh: Privately Printed, 1886.

Anonymous. *Midnight Horrors; or, The Bandit's Daughter: An Original Romance.* New York: W. Borradaile, 1823.

Reynolds, George W. M. *The Pixy; or, The Unbaptized Child: A Story for Christmas.* London: John Dicks, 1860?

Anonymous. *The Spectre Mother; or, The Haunted Tower.* New York: W. Borradaile, 1823.

Upton, Smyth. *The Last of the Vampires: A Tale.* Weston-Super-Mare, England: J. Whereat, The Columbian Press, 1845.
    Together with *R.I.P.*, this anthology covers one hundred years in the development of the supernatural novella, from the days of the gothic tale (1823) to the light ghost story of the twentieth century. All of the selections in this book originally appeared as separately published pamphlets.
    "The Spectre Mother" and "Midnight Horrors," both written by the same anonymous author, are rousing supernatural gothics in the traditional manner, set in mist-enshrouded castles, and featuring beautiful ladies, evil villains, and horrible spectres that serve the cause of justice.
    "The Demon Hunter" is a very early werewolf story, published anonymously in the mid-nineteenth century, possibly in the pages of some larger book or periodical. Hugo Krantz murders his wife and flees to the mountains; there he marries a beautiful girl who periodically turns into a wolf, and when he is forced to kill her to save his surviving son, the resulting curse pursues his family until they are all destroyed.
    "The Last of the Vampires" features the mysterious Baron Von Oberfels, a vampire who must kill a young girl every ten years to maintain his perpetual youth. In "A Nocturnal Expedition Round My Room," the narrator experiences an extraordinary vision. "The Pixy" is a ghost story in which the spirit of a child pursues its murderer until he makes amends. Count Albert von Sinnern, a German nobleman, falls in love with a witch's daughter, and then leaves her to marry another; the vindictive women curse the Count, and he later becomes "The Spectre Bridegroom."

Reginald, R., and Douglas Menville, editors. *They: Three Parodies of H. Rider Haggard's She.* New York: Arno Press, 1978.
CONTENTS:
Lang, Andrew, and Walter Herries Pollock, writing as "by the Author of 'It,' 'King Solomon's Wives,' 'Bess,' 'Much Darker Days,' 'Mr. Morton's Subtler' and Other Romances." *He.* London: Longmans, Green, 1887.

De Morgan, John. *He: A Companion to She: Being a History of the Adventures of J. Theodosius Aristophano on the Island of Rapa Nui in Search of His Immortal Ancestor.* New York: Norman L. Munro, 1887.

De Morgan, John. *"It": A Wild, Weird History of Marvelous, Miraculous, Phantasmagorical Adventures in Search of He, She, and Jess, and Leading to the Finding of "It": A Haggard Conclusion.* New York: Norman L. Munro, 1887.

Haggard's classic novel of lost-race adventure, *King Solomon's Mines*, was a sensation when published in 1885. He followed up that initial success with an even greater hit, *She*, a classic novel of an immortal white woman resident in the dim reaches of unknown Africa. *She* inspired no less than five different parodies, the three that are included in this volume, and two non-fantasy pastiches by Jacob Ralph Abarbanell, *Ma* and *Pa*, published by Norman L. Munro in 1887 after the success of *He* and *It*. As with the parodies *of King Solomon's Mines*, some bibliographical confusion exists because of similarities in titles.

The two novels by John De Morgan were issued in April of 1887, several months after the publication of the Lang/Pollock collaboration. All were issued anonymously, and, as was the case with the Hyder Ragged parody, the British edition of *He* had several American editions from the same publisher that produced the De Morgan versions. But they are quite different books in every respect. In fact, both *He: A Companion to She* and *It* feature the same character, J. Theodosius Aristophano, and may be considered for most purposes as a single novel, having been released almost simultaneously. This anthology represents the first time that these three parodies have been reprinted in a single, permanent edition.

Reynolds, George W. M. *The Necromancer: A Romance.* London: John Dicks, 1857.

For 134 years the accursed House of Danvers has preyed upon the innocent hearts of unsuspecting women: five different girls have given their souls to Danvers men, and each has vanished on the night preceding her nuptials.

On each occasion the remaining family members have sworn vengeance, but the name of Danvers apparently provides immunity from harm: pistols fired at point-blank range have no effect, swords are easily turned aside by a light foil, and six brawny men are humbled by the slender frame of one Danvers. The almost inhuman beauty of the Danvers men has never failed to conquer the object of their desire, until Musidora Sinclair refuses Lord Lionel Danvers in the year 1516. Lionel exacts his revenge, when he appears before the girl as King Henry VIII, who is known to be dissatisfied with his wife, Catherine of Aragon.

Henry proposes a secret marriage, and Dora accepts, with the King promising to reveal the union when the political climate is ripe. But shortly after the marriage is consummated, the real King, warned by Cardinal Wolsey, suddenly appears on the scene, and the bogus Henry changes into Lionel Danvers. Musidora bears the resulting child in secret, giving her up to foster parents, and later returns to her home on the Isle of Wight, and marries her childhood sweetheart, Percy Rivers.

But time is running short for the House of Danvers. In 1382, Walter Danvers had made a pact with the devil, receiving youth, good looks, money, and supernatural powers in exchange for the souls of six virgins freely given during the next 150 years. Throughout that period, Danvers had changed his name and appearance at will, but had only managed to obtain five of the souls he needed; should he fail to get the sixth before the time expires, he knows the devil will claim his own soul in forfeit. His last victim is Marian Musgrave, who is seduced by "Conrad" Danvers, and is taken by him to his castle on Wight on the last day of his term. With the midnight deadline approaching, Musidora suddenly appears on the scene, and proclaims the girl as Danvers's own daughter. The peer reels back in horror at his own iniquity, and is overwhelmed by a vast rushing of wings. The devil has taken back his own.

Rohmer, Sax. *Grey Face*. London: Cassell, 1924.

Sax Rohmer became one of the world's most widely read and highly paid writers of popular fiction during the

1920s and 1930s. His books, particularly the famous Fu Manchu series, have sold by the millions, been translated into over a dozen languages, and have served as the bases for countless motion picture, radio, television, and comic strip adaptations. Throughout his long and lively career, Rohmer maintained a serious interest in, and developed a thorough knowledge of, the occult. During the early 1900s he was a member of several occult societies, including the famous Hermetic Order of the Golden Dawn, whose membership included such names as William Butler Yeats, Arthur Machen, Charles Williams, Algernon Blackwood, Dion Fortune and Aleister Crowley. In 1914 Rohmer published a comprehensive history of magic, *The Romance of Sorcery*, which has also been reprinted.

Many of his novels and short stories draw upon this background of arcane knowledge with excellent effect; one of the most successful of these is *Grey Face*, a novel of mystery and the occult which Rohmer's biographers, Cay Van Ash and Elizabeth Sax Rohmer, have called: "...from the literary point of view, quite outstanding. Readers in the mid-1920s liked plots which were complex, and that of *Grey Face* is so intricate that it requires the closest attention to follow it. As an example of fashions in popular literature during that period, I consider it one of the finest things written." The plot concerns a man who has managed to obtain illegally terrible occult powers, using them to control the lives of a group of people around him, and the even more terrible fate that ultimately befalls him when occult retribution finally occurs.

Rolfe, Fr., and Harry Pirie-Gordon, writing as Prospero and Caliban. *Hubert's Arthur: Being Certain Curious Documents Found Among the Literary Remains of Mr. N. C.* London: Cassell, 1935.

That strange man known as Baron Corvo (his real name was Frederick Rolfe) wrote several equally bizarre novels, including his best-known work, *Hadrian VII*, in which Rolfe lived out his fantasies of becoming pope. *Hubert's Arthur*, published posthumously in 1935, is an alternate history in which Prince Arthur, son of Prince Geoffrey and nephew to King Richard the Lion-hearted and his presumed heir until John Lackland usurped the throne, manages to escape his real-life destiny of death by the hands of his nefarious uncle. Arthur becomes first the King of Jerusalem and then the King of England in succession to John. After conquering the Holy Land by marriage to Lady Mariolanthe, daughter of the queen of that land, he consolidates his rule and then invades England with the help of the King of France. John is defeated, and Arthur is anointed King of England, but is then challenged in single combat by Prince Henry, son of John. In a pitched battle, Arthur defends his God-given right and kills the prince with a massive sweep of his sword. He reigns in glorious splendor for many years until his apocalyptic death, when he is succeeded by his grandson, Prince Edward. Once again Rolfe has produced a novel which can truly be called fantastic.

Rosny, J. H., *Aîné*, translated by George Edgar Slusser. *The Xipéhuz; and, The Death of the Earth (Les Xipéhuz; et, La Mort de la terre).* New York: Arno Press, 1978.

J. H. Rosny, *Aîné* is rightly regarded as one of the leading French science-fiction and fantasy writers of the early part of the twentieth century; indeed, many critics have ranked him second only to Verne in his influence on French fantastic literature. And yet, this enormously imaginative writer has been virtually ignored by the English-speaking world, and only a few of his many books have been translated into other languages. Here are two of his short novels presented for the first time in an English translation.

The Xipéhuz features a tribe of nomads in a Babylonian setting. In their evolution to an agricultural state they are menaced by a race of intelligent aliens from the mineral kingdom. The story recounts attempts by a scientifically inclined human, Bakhoun, to understand this bizarre intelligence. He studies the "Forms" and finally is able to destroy them, not without misgivings for humanity, which passes from an age of innocence into a world that now knows darkness as well as light.

The Death of the Earth is a lost-race novel in reverse. The last men on earth are reduced to a precarious existence in a handful of oases, on a planet now drying out and being shaken by seismic spasms. A further menace is a race of "Terromagnetic" entities, now naturally on the rise in the evolutionary scheme of things as mankind wanes. The story revolves around the last heroic stirrings (and vain dreams) of an otherwise resigned and fatalistic humanity. The disaster is less man's fault than the natural course of events. Both of these books reflect Rosny's roots in nineteenth-century science and geology.

Russell, W. Clark. *The Death Ship: A Strange Story.* London: Hurst & Blackett, 1888.

In 1796 Geoffrey Fenton sails on the good ship *Saracen* as her second mate. Near the Cape of Good Hope, the crew spies a boat set out with archaic rigging, a strangely shaped hull, and many signs of external decay, including a flickering light that seems to permeate the craft. The superstitious sailors shout that it's the *Braave*, The Flying Dutchman, doomed to roam the seas forever because Vanderdecken, its master, had cursed the Almighty 143 years before for sending him ill winds. Fenton leans over the railing to get a better view, but suddenly loses his balance, and is picked up by the crew of the cursed vessel.

The men of the *Braave* have the appearance of walking dead: cold, pale skins, impassive features, without emotions or any human feelings. Like the ship, they have been preserved far beyond the span normally allotted to mere flesh. Their last memories are of the year 1653, and each time they attempt to round the Cape and are thrown back, they still believe the next time will be the last. Also on board is a young human girl, Imogene Dudley, who had been picked up from a shipwreck five years earlier.

Geoffrey and the girl fall in love, and plot their escape. During a great storm, the ship springs a leak, and Vanderdecken puts in to the African coast for repairs. That night, during a thick fog, the lovers steal one of the ship's boats, and flee the cursed boat. But the great-bearded captain fires blindly into the dark, and Imogene is fatally wounded by a stray bullet. Fenton is left to drift aimlessly with the body of his loved one, until a ship comes across the small boat weeks later. The sailor is saved, and tells his story to any who will listen. This is one of the best renditions of this ancient myth of the seas.

Russell, W. Clark. *The Frozen Pirate.* London: Sampson Low, Marston, Searle & Rivington, 1887, 2 vols.

This early novel of suspended animation takes place at sea. Paul Rodney, mate of the brig *Laughing Mary*, is the only survivor of a storm which capsizes the ship on a huge iceberg in the Antarctic. The block of ice continues to drift south with its unwilling passenger, and Rodney's plight seems hopeless, when he comes upon an old pirate ship locked tight in the ice fields.

Aboard the pirate vessel Rodney finds several rough-looking pirates frozen stiff, and ample stocks of food, drink, and coal. One of the sailors shows signs of life after being placed near an open fire, and the amazed mate massages his limbs, gradually bringing him to consciousness. The pirate, whose name is Jules Tassard, is astounded to find himself restored, and refuses to believe that he has been frozen for nearly fifty years. In gratitude, he shows Rodney several treasure chests stowed in the hold, but becomes harsh and surly when he learns that the ship is still stuck fast. The pirate becomes increasingly dangerous with inaction, and Rodney now wishes he had never revived him. Suddenly, the frozen sailor begins to age rapidly as the full weight of his 103 years catches up with him, and within the week he is dead. Rodney manages to free the boat, and with his treasure safely in hand returns to England a rich man.

"Sarban," pseud. of John W. Wall. *Ringstones and Other Curious Tales.* London: Peter Davies, 1951.

The long title story occupies most of this fine collection. Daphne Hazel has been engaged by Dr. Ravelin as a governess for some children staying with him at his estate, Ringstones. The old mansion is located in a valley buried deep within the lonely moors of the North Country, miles from civilization. The young people are delightful in many ways, but there are strange aspects to their characters that Daphne finds difficult to understand. Nuaman, the adolescent boy, is always running and playing, never standing still even for a moment; his vitality and energy are almost inhuman at times. And the two girls, Marvan and Ianthe, speak little English, yet Daphne is unable to determine where precisely they come from, and why they're staying with Dr. Ravelin.

In her dreams the governess sometimes sees the estate as it might have been in Roman times, with charioteers and athletes competing for prizes on an ancient track that encircles the valley. Then one night the dream becomes a reality when Nuaman suddenly becomes the godlike director of the games. He has just ordered Daphne to take her place on his chariot when she wakes up, and finds herself in the ruins of the decaying house. Her real-life employer, Dr. Hancock, had taken her out for a hike on the moors, and when she had sprained her ankle, had left her in the doorway of the mansion while he went for help. Daphne had fainted after hearing the whisperings and footsteps of unseen people just behind her, and had seemingly dreamt the entire story in Hancock's absence. And yet, the moors are a strange and lonely place, and there are stories of fairy bands who enchant humans left to wander alone. Later, one of Daphne's friends finds her broken watch band in the old stable-house at Ringstones. But, as Hancock points out, the injury to her ankle would have made it impossible for her to walk more than a few steps from the mysterious house. Also included in this book are the tales "A Christmas Story," "Capra," "Calmahain," and "The Khan."

Savile, Frank. *Beyond the Great South Wall: The Secret of the Antarctic*. London: Sampson Low, Marston, Searle & Rivington, 1899.

Jack Dorinecourte, an ex-British soldier, learns that he has succeeded to the title of his uncle, Viscount Heatherslie, who had been doing archaeological research in Central America. Heatherslie leaves a strange testament, urging his nephew to pursue his dream of finding the lost Antarctic land which the Mayas had supposedly settled when the Spaniards invaded their tribal domains. Jack and his friend Gerry Carver decide to mount an expedition in conjunction with the French archaeologist Professor Lessaution, and they head south to Antarctic waters. The barriers of rock and ice seem insurmountable until a timely eruption of volcanic forces flings them over the wall.

But the Indians are long since dead and gone, leaving fragmentary ruins, a few dead and frozen bodies, and some enigmatic signs leading to their treasury, which is filled with gold and jewels. There are also indications that the pagans worshiped a strange god, who suddenly appears as the last of a race of flesh-eating dinosaurs. It looks as if the intrepid party of adventurers is doomed to be sacrificed to the monster's gaping jaws, but the volcano suddenly decides to erupt again, this time in force, and it's all they can do to launch their ship and escape with their lives. The giant reptile is defeated by the forces of nature, and Jack and Gerry return to the more civilized clime of England.

Scott, G. Firth. *The Last Lemurian: A Westralian Romance*. London: James Bowden, 1898.

The Hatter tells Dick Halwood that in the middle of the Australian desert lies a strange land where there are piles of gold for the taking, and a strange yellow woman who rules a band of wizened pygmies. So Halwood and his new-found friend set out across untrodden wastes and the bleak reaches of waterless desert, where even the Aborigines fear to tread. Their water is nearly exhausted, when they spy a bluff in the distance and a small oasis at its base, fed by a waterfall dropping over the nearly sheer cliffs. After having refreshed themselves, they examine their surroundings, but other than trees and grass, there is no one around and no obvious way to reach the mountain fastness. As a precaution, they climb into a large tree overhanging the pool at the base of the cliff.

That night a door opens up in the rock, and a tall, majestic woman, glowing with a yellow sheen, approaches the pond with her attendants. The Hatter pretends he's the spirit of the night and convinces her that he is her long-lost lover, returning in reincarnated form. For Tor Ymmothe is the last Queen of Lemuria, who has been condemned to survive thousands of years alone in her hollowed-out caves to pay for the sins of her race, which was destroyed for its arrogance. She guards the sleeping body of a beautiful young princess, who has lain in a coma for thousands of years waiting for her own companion to return.

Halwood finds the receptacle where her body lies and is startled to recognize the face of a girl who had appeared in a vision more than a year before. When he opens the casket, her body revives briefly, just long enough for her to tell him to seek her soul somewhere in the outside world; then it crumbles away to dust. Suddenly, the volcano erupts, and the queen, the Hatter, and the remnants of Lemuria are destroyed. But Halwood escapes with his life and some wealth, returning to his English estate. When he searches out the Hatter's orphan daughter, he finds in her the living vision of his beloved, thus fulfilling the ancient prophecy.

Seaborn, Captain Adam, pseud. *Symzonia: A Voyage of Discovery*. New York: J. Seymour, 1820.

This was the first of the hollow-earth books, as well as the first American utopia. Capt. Seaborn tells the story of a strange voyage into an inner world. In 1817 he prepares an ocean-going steamship to test the theories of John Cleves Symmes, who earlier that year had proposed that the interior of the Earth is hollow, and that access to the inner lands could be gained through holes in the polar caps. Seaborn sails south, and encounters pack ice below the Falkland Islands. As the *Explorer* swings eastward to bypass the ice, the pack suddenly breaks away, and disappears altogether as they move south and east. There they find an unknown continent, which the captain calls Seaborn's Land after himself.

After leaving a party to winter on the coast, the ship continues on its course, and soon reaches open sea. The compass starts turning in circles, and the sun is now straight overhead, a sure sign the explorers have entered the internal world. Land is sighted, and Seaborn calls the new realm Symzonia. The Symzonians are much superior to the outer worlders. They never forget anything they learn. Their government is ruled by the best and most honorable men of the realm. War and murder and crimes of any sort are outlawed.

150

Incorrigibles are exiled to an island near the north polar entrance to their world.

Seaborn discovers that the men of the outer world are descended from these corrupt degenerates, and tries to hide this from his hosts. But the Symzonians translate the English books carried on the *Explorer,* and are horrified by what they find. The outsiders must leave, lest their barbaric ways influence the young. Seaborn and his men return home, and in a series of mishaps, lose their specimens and manuscripts. The Captain himself is ruined when his broker goes bankrupt, and now, to help pay his debts, he is writing this narrative to mount another expedition to the inner world.

Sheldon-Williams, Miles. *The Power of Ula.* London: Ward, Lock, 1906.

Here is a fast-paced, action-filled lost-race novel of the type that A. Merritt was later to write so well. Three young Englishmen, soldiers at heart, Bob Wilmot, Patrick McDiarmid, and the narrator of the tale, Richard Langley, are enlisted in the service of a beautiful and mysterious woman named Ula Valdien. She claims to be the wrongfully exiled heir to the throne of a lost kingdom of South Americans called the Valdi, an offshoot of the Aztecs and survivors from the destruction of Atlantis. They are the legendary Amazons, and their matriarchal society has worshipped the goddess Artaven and her terrible Golden Snake for four centuries, until a rival faction overthrew and exiled Ula, the rightful Queen-Empress.

Although Bob and Richard notice a streak of cruelty in Ula and are a bit skeptical, Patrick is completely smitten with her and becomes her total slave. After a long sea voyage on a ship loaded with modern armaments and an arduous trek through impenetrable jungle, the party reaches the ancient and secret land of the Valdi. They are met by the Lady Valma, current ruler and a beautiful and gracious woman who reveals to Bob and Richard the true story—that Ula is a usurper, champion of an evil religion that demands human sacrifice.

The two men believe Valma and switch their allegiance to her, but Patrick, hopelessly in love with Ula, chooses to go with her. A terrible series of bloody battles follows, the female warriors of Ula against those of Valma. Despite a valiant resistance, Valma's forces are eventually overwhelmed and the triumphant Ula prepares to offer the two Englishmen and Valma as sacrifices to the hideous living Golden Snake she controls. But a fierce storm arises and the idol of Artaven is destroyed by lightning! The great snake, mad with fear, kills Ula and dies. The reign of terror is over and the Lady Valma and Bob, whom she has come to love, will lead her people once more into the light.

Shiel, M. P. *The Lord of the Sea.* London: Grant Richards, 1901.

The Jews have been expelled from Europe, and have taken refuge in England, where they are becoming a major political and economic force. One Jewish financier, Baruch Frankl, is insulted by Richard Hogarth, and in revenge deprives him of his savings, frames him on a murder charge, and puts his sister in a sanatorium. But Hogarth escapes from prison, and acting on a tip from one of his cellmates, finds a large diamond meteorite on Frankl's English estate. By selling his diamonds, Hogarth becomes one of the world's richest men, and he begins building a series of floating forts designed to his own specifications. Each of these behemoths is placed strategically in the center of a major shipping lane, where they soon become accepted features of the ocean landscape.

Suddenly, however, a large new passenger liner is ordered to stop dead in the water, and pay a tax to the Lord of the Sea before proceeding on to its destination. The ship's captain refuses, and his boat is blown out of the water. The major nations of the world mount a fleet to bring this upstart under control, and return control of the seas to the world, but the battleships and cruisers cannot withstand Hogarth's terrible weapons. All the countries of the earth must now acknowledge his control of the waters. Richard is made Regent of Great Britain, and orders the Jews deported to the new land he has made for them in Palestine. As they begin departing, Frankl arranges for the sea forts to be destroyed by treachery, and Richard himself is nearly assassinated on the old Jew's orders. In a final blow, the now powerless Regent discovers his father was really a Jew, and he leaves (under his own orders) for the resurrected Israel, where he marries Frankl's daughter, and is elected Judge of the new country by its inhabitants.

Sicard, Clara. *The Ghost: A Legend.* London: Chas. H. Clark, 1866?

This early supernatural classic tells the story of Cedric of the Left Hand, who followed Richard Coeur de Lion to Palestine on the crusade. In the course of his adventures, Cedric rescues a holy man from a band of brigands, and the old man promises the knight that, as a reward, he will be able to return from the dead to help his family on two occasions in the future.

The Barons Trevanion prosper over the centuries, and by 1644 have gathered great estates in England. But the present Baron is being besieged in his castle by the soldiers of King Charles I. The nobleman's son, Percy, is married to the niece of Lord Essex, a supporter of Cromwell. The situation is becoming desperate, when Cedric appears, disguised as Geoffrey, a falconer who had died ten years previously. Geoffrey convinces the baron and his son that all will be lost unless they reconcile the Trevanion honor with King Charles, and Margaret prepares to hand the castle over to the king's forces. Prince Rupert, commander of the Cavaliers, is determined to destroy his old enemies, and Cedric/Geoffrey saves the trio by leading them through a secret passage to his tomb. Trevanion is reconciled with his king, and the line is saved.

. A hundred years later, the family's fortunes rest with Reginald II, Duke of Trevanion. Reginald is enamored of an unworthy actress, Mlle. Fiordiligi, and is banished for his indiscretions by the king. His blind stubbornness also causes pain to Lady Cecilia Beauchamp, a wealthy heiress who loves him dearly. In addition to these problems, other complications with the estate have surfaced: an old unpaid debt suddenly comes due, and the receipt discharging the amount has mysteriously disappeared. Cedric returns again, as an old lover of Fiordiligi, and convinces the harlot that her future happiness lies with the stage. Cecilia secretly substitutes herself for the actress in the marriage ceremony, making herself Duchess of Trevanion. Cedric then produces the missing document, and Reginald finds that he has really loved Cecilia all along.

Sinclair, Upton. *Prince Hagen: A Phantasy*. Boston: L. C. Page, 1903.

Upton Sinclair lived a long and productive life as an author. At the beginning of his career, before publication of his famous classic on the working class, *The Jungle*, Sinclair wrote several novels on various topics, including one fantasy, *Prince Hagen.*

The narrator is listening to Richard Wagner's "Das Rheingold" when he is swept away by a hoard of little creatures into Nibelheim, the underground world of German myth and legend. There King Alberich gives him an onerous chore: the education of his unruly grandson, Prince Hagen, who is still a young man, just 800 years old. Hagen is petty and cruel, but he sets out to learn the ways of earthly civilization and master the lessons taught by society. He sets his sights on a political career by becoming a street orator for Tammany Hall, and then immediately switches sides, exposing the political machinations of the Democrats, and ingratiating himself with the Republicans.

King Alberich dies, and with the immense wealth Hagen has inherited, he becomes the mainstay of New York society, throwing massive social events at his mansion in Newport. To advance his position, Hagen becomes engaged to a beautiful debutante, and is preparing to expand his influence when his carriage bolts, and he is thrown to the ground and killed. New York is aghast at this tragedy, and Hagen's death is celebrated in the most expensive funeral ever given in the city. Sinclair uses his satirical pen to the fullest, slashing away at the conventions of his time and anticipating his later, more serious critiques of capitalistic society.

A Stable for Nightmares; or, Weird Tales. New York: New Amsterdam Book Co., 1896.

This anonymously edited anthology contains eleven superb stories of the macabre: "Dickon the Devil," by J. Sheridan Le Fanu, tells of the strange haunting of Barwyke Hall by the mysterious Squire Bowes. "Devereux's Dream" reveals a murder years before it actually happens. Sir Charles Young's tale, "A Debt of Honor," is a story of vengeance exacted from beyond the grave by a murdered youth. In "Catherine's Quest," a young girl sees a vision of a foul murder committed two hundred years earlier, and is restored to her rightful heritage as a result. "Haunted" tells how the spirit of a murdered man seeks help in a Southern inn to gain revenge upon his murderer.

"What Was It?" is Fitz-James O'Brien's classic tale of a hideous invisible creature which suddenly appears from nowhere, and is captured after it attacks the narrator. "Pichon and Sons, of the Croix Rousse," tells the story of a young noble during the French Revolution who promises his lover that he will return, alive or dead. In "The Phantom Fourth," a group of three compatriots on a vacation in France suddenly find their gatherings haunted by a mysterious phantom who continually gets them into trouble. "The Spirit's Whisper" urges a man to punish his lover's killer. "Dr. Feversham's Story" tells how a family haunting that augurs death appears just prior to the wedding of a favorite daughter. In "Two Plaster Casts," a hanged murderer is cast in plaster by a sculptor to provide him with verisimilitude in his work.

Stevens, Francis. *The Heads of Cerberus*. Reading, PA: Polaris Press, 1952.

Gertrude Bennett, the mysterious woman who wrote under the pen name "Francis Stevens," has been called the greatest female fantasy writer between Mary Wollstonecraft Shelley and C. L. Moore. During a short seven-year period, she produced both novels and short stories for such early pulp magazines as *Argosy*, *All-Story Weekly*, and *The Thrill Book*. Absolutely nothing about her or her background was known for many years; she was thought by some to be A. Merritt writing under a pseudonym because of the fine quality of her work.

In 1923 her final tale, "Sunfire," was published in *Weird Tales*; after that, "Francis Stevens" disappeared from the scene. She had been a secretary before commencing her writing career to support herself and her infant daughter after the accidental death of her husband, and she had again returned to secretarial work. In 1939 mystery again surrounded Gertrude Bennett—she vanished without a trace! She left behind several outstanding novels: *Claimed*, *Citadel of Fear*, and *The Heads of Cerberus*. Unfortunately, these works had to wait many years before book publication: *Cerberus* initially appeared as a five-part serial in *The Thrill Book*, beginning in the August 15, 1919, issue, but was not put between hard covers until a deluxe, limited, boxed edition was published by Polaris Press in 1952.

Although *Cerberus* is more of a science-fiction novel than most of her others, it nevertheless contains strong and tantalizing fantasy elements. A group of people is transported by a mysterious substance called "The Dust of Purgatory" into a strange world of shadow-beings and a white goddess, the Weaver of the Years. The Weaver sends them forward in time to an alternate Philadelphia of the future, now under tyrannical rule. After rebelling against the rulers, the group manages to return to their own time and dimension. This novel was the first to envisage the parallel time-track concept, with the unique added idea of a time difference between the two worlds.

Taine, John. *Before the Dawn.* Baltimore: Williams & Wilkins Co., 1934.

John Taine, a noted mathematician and scientist under his real name, Eric Temple Bell, attempts a realistic recreation of life in the Age of Reptiles. Professor Sellar discovers a means of extracting the light which has been absorbed by material objects during the course of their history, thus enabling scientists to project visual scenes from prehistoric times into an arena. With the proper rocks, organic substances, or other surviving relics, the archaeologist or paleontologist can now examine actual "televisor" records from any part of the Earth's history. Sellar is particularly interested in examining the reasons for the extinction of the dinosaurs, and he begins sifting records from that period.

One creature in particular, an immense flesh-eater, attracts his attention; he names the animal Belshazzar, and attempts to follow it through its lengthy career. Changes in climate caused by widespread geologic upheavals and volcanic eruptions are beginning to affect the giant reptiles. The northern regions become colder as volcanic ash obscures the sun, and causes temperatures to drop rapidly during a short period of time. The great animals become sluggish in the cold, and find their normal food supplies disappearing. Those creatures unable to leave die of starvation or the cold; the rest head South towards the narrow bridge connecting North and South America. Only a few hundred reach the temperate climate of South America. The survivors fight among themselves for the limited food supply, and in the end the last two carnivores kill each other over a meal. The few remaining plant-eaters succumb to the ever-present volcanoes.

Todd, Ruthven. *Over the Mountain*. London: George G. Harrap, 1939.

Ruthven Todd was truly a man with a many-faceted talent: considered one of the foremost poets of the twentieth century, he was once a member of the Dylan Thomas circle; during the 1930s he was one of the leaders of the Surrealist movement, an influence which can be found to a large degree in his novel, *The Lost Traveller* (1943), and to a lesser degree in *Over the Mountain*, his first published novel. Todd was also one of the world's leading authorities on William Blake, and a well-known historian of science, particularly the world of early nineteenth-century Romantic science. He wrote about the genesis of this book:

> ...in 1938, under a suddenly renewed influence of Kafka and a good many others, I came to write the novel actually published earliest, *Over the Mountain*. *Over the Mountain* was conceived and written before I had read Rex Warner's *The Wild Goose Chase*, and I was, I

think, a little chagrined to realize that they both bore some evidence of the political atmosphere of the period of their adolescence. Looking back at them today, I can see how very different they are both in intent and in achievement. Obviously I had less political purpose, although I was one of the inert minnows in the political stream of that day.

The novel shows a strong Kafkaesque influence indeed, the story of a young man who lives in an unspecified village near the base of a high mountain, where no one has ever climbed or lived. Determined to cross over the mountain and explore the unknown region on the other side, the young man, Michael, barely survives the arduous climb; he eventually finds himself in a village much like the one he has left, as a curiosity and a hero. However, when he refuses to cooperate with the authorities or to be used for various religious and political purposes, he becomes a hunted criminal, hounded by the secret police and the mindless, imbecilic killers they employ. After many narrow escapes, Michael flees back over the mountain to his own village—or does he? Was he in his own village all the time? We are never sure in this biting and nightmarish allegory of the misuse and perversion of authority.

Train, Arthur, and Robert Williams Wood. *The Man Who Rocked the Earth*. Garden City, NY: Doubleday, Page & Co., 1915.

The Man Who Rocked the Earth contains an early discussion of atomic power, and the first description of radiation sickness. The First World War is at its height, and the warring nations threaten to reduce all of civilization to barbarism. A wireless message is received at the Washington Naval Observatory from a person calling himself Pax, who says he is able to control nature, and who promises to demonstrate his power by increasing the length of the sidereal day by five minutes. Subsequently, a strange yellow aurora is observed throughout the world, and small seismic tremors shake the globe. The astronomers confirm that the

Earth's rotation has been slowed down by the promised length of time. A second message warns the Earth that Pax is now the master of the world's destiny, and he orders the nations to cease fighting and destroy their weapons.

The leaders of the world insist upon a harmless demonstration of the dictator's powers, and the scientist replies by disrupting the Atlas Mountains in northern Africa, thereby flooding the Sahara desert from the Mediterranean Sea. A strange, ring-shaped aircraft is observed over the desert, projecting a lavender ray which contains sufficient power to destroy the Earth itself. The nations negotiate for peace, and an armistice is signed, but a fanatical German military commander breaks the accord by suddenly attacking Paris. Pax's reprisal is swift and terrible, as the violet ray decimates the German troops. Then, angered by this violation of his edict, the scientist threatens to shift the world's axis, and turn Europe into an Arctic wasteland. Meanwhile, Professor Benjamin Hooker, who has been performing experiments similar to those demonstrated by Pax, undertakes a long and arduous journey to track the madman to his lair. He arrives just in time to see the ray machine destroy itself and its inventor due to an accidental overload. The Flying Ring is still unharmed, and Hooker flies it back to the US.

Viereck, George Sylvester. *The House of the Vampire.* New York: Moffat, Yard, 1907.

The concept of the vampire is as old as recorded history, and appears in the legends and literature of almost every people on earth; but it was not until the publication in London of Bram Stoker's *Dracula* in 1897 that the image crystallized in the minds of the English-speaking world as a hideously pale, blood-drinking creature of the night with supernatural powers. Since then, this concept of the vampire has appeared as the most fearsome of all supernatural menaces in countless novels, stories, plays, motion pictures, comic books, and television dramas.

But George Sylvester Viereck, poet, editor, and novelist, wrote in his first novel of another kind of vampire. This being is, if anything, even more horrifying, for he is a psychic vampire with the occult power to absorb not blood, but the creative impulses and energies of the people who fall under his spell. Gradually, they become weaker and less creative, and the vampire—Reginald Clarke—becomes ever stronger and more brilliant. He is able to steal entire plays and novels from the minds of young writers, works not yet committed to paper, and claim them for himself. Cold, suave, world-acclaimed for his writings and wit, Clarke has only loved one woman in all his life—Ethel Brandenbourg, a promising young artist—but as he sapped the creativity from her mind, she lost her gift for color, while new brilliance suddenly appeared in Clarke's verses. Now she both hates and loves him, and tries to warn a young writer who falls in love with her that Clarke is stealing his ideas as he has countless others. As the young man confronts Clarke, the vampire brings the full force of his terrible magnetism into play, and the story rushes to a truly horrifying climax.

Vivian, E. Charles. *Aia: Fields of Sleep, and People of the Darkness*. New York: Arno Press, 1978.

E. Charles Vivian, curiously enough, is best known in the field of fantastic literature for his series of books on Gees, the London detective who has a penchant for getting mixed up in cases involving the occult forces of evil just beyond the fringes of everyday life. The Gees books were all published under the pseudonym Jack Mann. But Vivian had an earlier incarnation as a writer of fantastic adventure tales filled with bold adventure, daring escapades, and a strong romantic line. Two of his best lost-race books, which together form one continuous narrative, are *Fields of Sleep* and *People of the Darkness*, now republished in one volume for the first time.

Victor Marshall is sent by Madame Delarey to find her son Clement (who has inherited a fortune) on Sapelung, an island not far from Indonesia, where he had disappeared three years before. Journeying into the interior, Marshall comes to a strange formation that shows signs of human design. Before he has time to investigate, flesh-eating land crabs force him to jump down an incline that permits no return, and he is confronted by Tari-Hi, the keeper of the place. Mah-Eng is the last outpost of the ancient Babylonian Empire, a gold mine left when Babylon was destroyed. Its laborers are bound to the land by a strange flower that holds its victims enthralled by its exotic perfume; when deprived of the marvelous scent, the slaves soon die. Only the keepers are immune. Strangers are forced to remain, or are condemned to death.

Tari-Hi, who has no sons, wants Marshall to marry his beautiful daughter Aia and carry on the line, but Marshall declines. The artificial aqueduct carrying the river through the mine works is destroyed accidentally, the flowers are submerged by the overflowing waters, and the laborers die in their sleep. Clement Delarey, who had joined the colonists, is among the dead.

Vivian, E. Charles. *A King There Was—*. London: Hodder & Stoughton, 1926.

In Asuraten, men plot to overthrow the unpopular king, Antores; for his predecessor had sired a son by a herder's daughter, unknown to all but two of the king's men. When he died without legitimate issue, they had secreted the boy away, fearing that Antores would kill him to gain the throne so near his grasp. But now Ronal has become a strong young man, and discontent lends to the treason. Civil war is waged between the two kings, and Ronal conquers easily. Antores is killed by treachery, his daughter Niala is Queen for an hour, and Ronal is crowned in his place. But the northerners from Antores' part of the kingdom have not forgotten their shame, and they begin sending colonists south, building an insidious fifth column in the lower provinces. Five years later, the stage is set for revolt.

King Ronal has left for an inspection of the Northern provinces and the south is complacent in its peace. Meten, one of the transplanted northerners, gathers together an army and marches on the capital. But the king is informed, and the two armies meet at Tarasin. Meten is killed in the fray and Ronal prevails. Civil war has weakened Asuraten, and when plague breaks out, it seems as if the gods have frowned upon the land. Suddenly, little hairy barbarians invade from the north. The killing disease leaves too few men for defense, and one by one, the provinces are lost. It becomes clear that

ROBERT REGINALD & DOUGLAS MENVILLE

the only hope is to gather together the few remaining ships of
the fleet, and evacuate the hundreds or thousands still alive.
While Ronal and his soldiers hold off the hordes, the women
and children are hurried aboard the grain vessels. Ronal is
wounded in the final charge, but is carried off to the ship by
his men. In the eastern isles, they live out their days in
peace.

Vivian, E. Charles, writing as Jack Mann. *Maker of
Shadows.* London: Wright & Brown, 1938.
  No collection of supernatural fiction would be com-
plete without an example of the psychic detective at work.
Gregory George Gordon Green, called "Gees" by his friends,
seems to have a penchant for cases involved with the supernatural. He receives an urgent request for help from Margaret Aylener, and travels to her estate in Brachmornalachan,
Scotland. Margaret fears for the life of her niece, Helen, who
has been entranced by Gamel MacMorn.
  The MacMorns have been mortal enemies of the
Ayleners for untold centuries, and Gamel, the present scion
of the house, may himself be hundreds of years old. His
house, located just a few miles away, is built upon the remains of an ancient Druidic circle, said to have been made by
MacMorn's ancestors (and possibly by the sorcerer himself).
Margaret tells Gees that the disappearance of young girls
every forty years throughout the last century is somehow
connected with the magician's apparent immortality; that he
has used the lives of these unfortunate women to extend his
own beyond its normal span. And now he has his eyes on
Helen Aylener for the next part of the cycle.
  Gees agrees to take the case, and finds himself attacked on different occasions by swarms of flies, shadows,
and mysterious fogs and mists that appear out of a clear sky.
He determines to visit MacMorn in his own lair, but the ancient is waiting, and Gees is drugged. The ceremony of
transference begins, but the shadows of the sorcerer's previous victims wake the detective from his sleep, and he enters the stone circle just as the Unnamed begins to form the
giant figure of a woman with claws. A shot from his re-
volver disturbs the ceremony, and the spirit vanishes; Gamel

162

MacMorn slips into the burning oil, and becomes a writhing torch whose quick death releases the shadows of his victims to return to their souls. But Helen Aylener pines away in her home, part of her being lost forever, and dies shortly thereafter.

Wakefield, H. Russell. *Ghost Stories.* London: Jonathan Cape, 1932.

H. Russell Wakefield has a steady if limited following amongst aficionados of the English ghost story; Lovecraft once remarked that he "achieved great heights of horror despite a vitiating air of sophistication." This collection includes some of his best: "Messrs. Turkes and Talbot" deals with a publisher haunted by the partner he murdered; "A Peg on Which to Hang" tells of a hotel room which never gives one a good night's rest; before buying a "Used Car," Mr. Canning finds it's always well to determine why it's being sold; Agatha murders Uncle Samuel by helping his cold along with "Damp Sheets"—unfortunately, Uncle Samuel doesn't stay in his grave; "The Cairn" features a unique monster that only makes its appearance when the ground is covered with snow; in "Blind Man's Bluff," Mr. Cort decides to examine his new house after dark, a most regrettable decision.

"'Look Up There!'" tells the peculiar story of a house only haunted on New Year's Eve. Jim Brinton doesn't believe in ghosts, but "The Frontier Guards" change his mind. Horrocks rents "Mr. Ash's Studio" to do a little creative writing, and gets somewhat more than he bargained for. The "Nurse's Tale" relates the story of the Laytons' family curse. In a curious "Coincidence at Hunton," Bob Harriday kills his girlfriend, and is accidentally killed himself on the same spot a few months later. Mr. Rhode, the famous ghost story writer, creates a diabolical new piece featuring "The Red Hand," and finds his invention becoming real. In "An Echo," Robert sees a vision explaining an unsolved murder.

"Day-Dream in Macedon" is a ghost story of World War I. Fisherman Broadbent hears the tapping of trapped submariners in "Knock! Knock! Who's There?" Philip Purcell discovers a murderess with the help of vengeful spirits, but the real story is "An Epilogue by Roger Bantock." Also included are "The Last to Leave," "The Central Figure," "Old Man's Beard," "Present at the End," and "A Jolly Surprise for Henri."

Waterloo, Stanley. *The Story of Ab: A Tale of the Time of the Cave Man*. Chicago: Way & Williams, 1897.

Noted critic Thomas D. Clareson called this novel the prototype for all later prehistoric romances. Indeed, the most famous of the early cave man books, Jack London's *Before Adam* (1907), caused an international stir because of its obvious similarities to the Waterloo book. Ab is a Stone Age boy who grows to young manhood amid the many dangers of his time. With his friend, Oak, he digs a pit and catches a baby rhinoceros, participates in a mammoth hunt with the tribe to prove himself a man, and courts the young women from a neighboring tribe.

One girl in particular, Lightfoot, holds the attention of both men, and Ab is forced to kill his friend in a savage fight. He wins Lightfoot for his mate, but is haunted by guilt for his murdered companion. As Ab grows older, he helps the tribe kill a marauding saber-tooth tiger, leads his people in a great battle against an invading tribe, and eventually becomes the leader of the cave men, and the patriarch of a large personal family. Ab is used by the author to support his contention that there was no sharp division between the Paleolithic and Neolithic periods; man learned to make fine, polished tools and weapons gradually and naturally, as Ab does. During his life Ab invents and perfects the bow and arrow, and is the first of the primitives to domesticate wolves as pets.

Wells, H. G. *The Wonderful Visit*. London: J. M. Dent & Sons, 1895.

H. G. Wells has always been considered—quite properly so—a science-fiction writer, since the bulk of his nonrealistic fiction falls into the class of what he called, in 1902 "wild 'pseudo' scientific extravaganza." However, some thirty-odd years later, he came to view his work somewhat differently:

These tales have been compared with the work of Jules Verne.... As a matter of fact there is no literary resemblance whatever between the anticipatory inventions of the great Frenchman and these fantasies...these stories of mine collected here do not pretend to deal with possible things; they are exercises of the imagination in a quite different field. They belong to a class of writing which includes *The Golden Ass* of Apuleius, the *True Histories* of Lucian, *Peter Schlemihl*, and the story of *Frankenstein*.... They are all fantasies.

Today, we might disagree with Wells's appraisal of such works as *The Time Machine, The War of the Worlds*, and *The First Men in the Moon*, but he did write a few tales which are pure fantasy by anyone's definition. Sadly, many of these have been overshadowed by his more popular works; *The Wonderful Visit* is such a novel. It was his third novel, written after *The Island of Dr. Moreau* but published before it, and is a bittersweet, tragicomic story of an angel who somehow "falls to earth" from his angelic dimension, and is totally unable to adapt to the hypocrisy and petty pomposity of society in a small English village. His pure and natural appearance and reactions to people and events soon earn him the stern enmity of the villagers, with only the brave and loyal Vicar his friend. The angel becomes more and more human (and correspondingly miserable), falls in love with a serving girl, and finally sacrifices his life to save her from a burning house. But she too dies and their souls unite in ecstasy at last, freed from the dreary, unenlightened world of humanity.

White, Stewart Edward, and Samuel Hopkins Adams. *The Mystery*. New York: McClure, Phillips, 1907.
Two of the more popular novelists of the early 1900s join forces to produce a science-fiction adventure that Dr. Thomas D. Clareson has called "one of the best-written [SF

novels] of the period." The *USS Wolverine,* a cruiser on duty in the South Pacific, comes upon the deserted schooner *Laughing Lady,* which has been missing at sea for two years. No one can be found on board the ship, but a heavy, locked metal chest is located in the cabin. The schooner becomes separated from the cruiser in the fog, with several seamen still on board. The warship observes a weird, multicolored light in the distance, and when the schooner is sighted again, the seamen have disappeared. More men are sent to the lost ship, but the schooner drifts away, and cannot be located again.

Several days later, the *Wolverine* picks up a half-dead man in a dory. His name is Ralph Slade, and he relates an incredible story. The renowned physicist, Dr. Schermerhorn, and his assistant, Percy Darrow, chartered the schooner to take them to an unknown volcanic island, where the Doctor could complete his search for a source of ultimate energy. After many months of research, he succeeded in isolating a fantastic substance called "celestium," which was vastly more powerful than radium, and capable of transmuting the elements. But the villainous crew, thinking the scientist was making gold, mutinied, killing the captain and Schermerhorn. The volcano erupted, and the crew fled in the ship with the Doctor's chest. Darrow was forced to remain on the island. When the crew attempted to open the chest, the radiation inside destroyed them, and only Slade managed to escape in the dory.

The captain of the *Wolverine* believes the journalist's story, and proceeds to the volcanic island, where Darrow is rescued. Darrow then completes the tale, and the mystery of the disappearing seamen is finally solved.

Whiting, Sydney. *Heliondé; or, Adventures in the Sun.* London: Chapman & Hall, 1855.

Benedict is sun-bathing one afternoon when he is literally dissolved by its potent rays, and is swept away towards the great orb in the sky. There he assumes colossal bodily form, and finds that the sun is inhabited by semi-spiritual beings of great wisdom and beauty. Near the capital city of Heliopolis he is met by his guide, Alutedon, who escorts him to his new residence, already prepared in advance. Heliophilus, as he is now called, is introduced to the prince of the realm, Helionax, who by virtue of his position (and vice versa) is the wisest, most virtuous, and most handsome of the sun's inhabitants. His wife, Heliotrope, is similarly the most beautiful woman, and the narrator soon succumbs to her charms, despite the attention of the princess's sister, Heliosweet.

Heliophilus commissions a sculpture from a master craftsman that is so faithful to the original that he spends all of his time worshiping the idol in his garden. Suddenly the cold piece of stone seems to come alive, and he professes his love. But the figure is actually Heliosweet, now transformed by her love for the earthman into a mirror image of her sister. The two exchange their vows, and live happily until Heliophilus expresses a desire to return to his native planet. With his new wife at his side, the earthman is swept back into space; as they near the green planet, the narrator resumes his original form, and Heliosweet is transformed into the image of Christabel, Benedict's former fiancée. He wakes up on the exact spot where he left the planet, wondering whether his travels were only a dream, or whether he really did travel to the wondrous world of Heliondé.

Wicks, Mark. *To Mars Via the Moon: An Astronomical Story*. London: Seeley & Co., 1911.

To Mars Via the Moon is an excellent example of the scientific story used for instruction; it is filled with the then-latest astronomical findings concerning both the Moon and Mars, and includes several charts. Particular emphasis is placed on the theories of Dr. Percival Lowell, one of the foremost astronomers of his day, and a major proponent of the idea that the Martian canals were constructed by intelligent beings.

A young scientist, John Yiewsley Claxton, his foster father, Wilfred Poynders, and their engineer, Kenneth M'Allister, embark on a journey to the planet Mars in an airship powered by Claxton's advanced electrical and magnetic engines. They pass close to the Moon's surface, but decide to continue on their travels without landing. Upon reaching

Mars, the explorers are cordially welcomed by the Martians, a handsome, gentle human race averaging seven feet in height. The Martians live in a utopian society, utilizing great canals to irrigate their arid world, and communicating across great distances by means of telepathy.

Poynders is astounded to find his deceased son reincarnated in the body of a Martian named Merna, and the great secret of the Martians is revealed; after death, each soul is re-embodied on another planet. Poynders, who has spent his entire life studying Mars, decides to remain on the planet with his "son," while Claxton and M'Allister return home. Back on Earth, Claxton's wild story is totally unaccepted, and his relatives conspire to have him declared insane and put away so they can inherit the money left to him by Poynders. But he is saved by a sympathetic friend of great influence, and his story is finally accepted with great enthusiasm by astronomers and scientists everywhere.

Wright, S. Fowler. *Deluge: A Romance; and, Dawn*. New York: Arno Press, 1975. Originally published in 1928 and 1928, respectively.

A great cataclysm shakes the world, and much of Great Britain sinks beneath the ocean during a terrifying windstorm that has already flattened most of mankind's dwellings. Martin Webster and his wife, Helen, manage to survive that first horrible night, but become separated as waves of salt water come surging into the English countryside. Webster, believing his wife drowned, moves into an old railway tunnel, which provides some shelter from the elements, and manages to scavenge some of the remnants of civilization. While down by the shores of the new sea, he sees a woman stagger out of the waves after swimming miles from some outlying island. Claire moves in with Martin, but is kidnapped by a band of twenty renegades who mean to use her as a common mistress for the group. Webster manages to rescue her, but the pair are besieged in their tunnel until a second group, headed by Tom Aldworth, attacks the outlaws.

Aldworth's band is attempting to preserve some semblance of civilization in a chaotic world, and has built a small settlement in the northern part of the island, about twenty miles away. The renegades represent a threat to their budding community that must be put down. After destroying the outlaws, the northern men make Webster their permanent leader, and are on their way home when they learn that a third group of survivors under Jerry Cooper is attacking their unprotected homestead. Webster and his men arrive in time to drive off the marauders with losses, but Martin finds that his wife and children are alive and well in the new community. Under the laws of the settlement, both Helen and Claire choose Webster for their husband. But this policy causes difficulties in a world where few women have survived. Webster's opponents rebel, and join forces with Cooper, who has been biding his time in the wilderness. Webster leads a cavalry charge that destroys the outlaws, and Cooper is killed. Peace is re-established, and Martin now leads his colony towards the building of a new and hopefully better world.

INDEX